"YOU'RE DYING, FLETCHER, RIGHT WHERE YOU STAND..."

Pickett's voice carried over the entire parade ground, electrifying all who heard.

Fletcher stared at Pickett. The only chance for Fletcher and the other two was to push their way clear with their hostages.

"You're gonna get these officers killed," said Fletcher.

"They ain't *my* officers," said Pickett. "The only thing that meant anything to me was my family, Fletcher. And for what you did to them, all of you are going to die."

Kincaid, Conway, and Cohen flung themselves forward. At the same time, Pickett's red-hot hatred was bringing his guns out and up like greased lightning...

EASY COMPANY

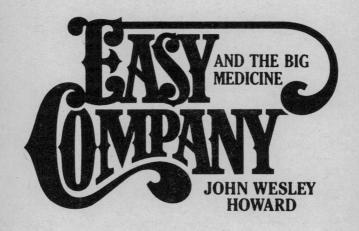

EASY COMPANY
AND THE BIG MEDICINE

JOHN WESLEY HOWARD

For information address: Jove Publications, Inc., 200 Madison Avenue, New York, New York 10016.

First Jove edition published July 1981

First printing

Printed in the United States of America

Jove books are published by Jove Publications, Inc., 200 Madison Avenue, New York, NY 10016

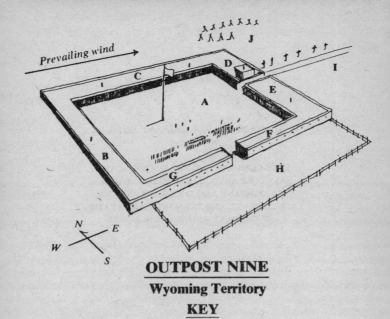

OUTPOST NINE

Wyoming Territory

KEY

A. Parade and flagstaff

B. Officers' quarters ("officers' country")

C. Enlisted men's quarters: barracks, day room, and mess

D. Kitchen, quartermaster supplies, ordnance shop, guardhouse

E. Suttler's store and other shops, tack room, and smithy

F. Stables

G. Quarters for dependents and guests; communal kitchen

H. Paddock

I. Road and telegraph line to regimental headquarters

J. Indian camp occupied by transient "friendlies"

INTERIOR   OUTSIDE

OUTPOST NUMBER NINE
(DETAIL)

Outpost Number Nine is a typical High Plains military outpost of the days following the Battle of the Little Big Horn, and is the home of Easy Company. It is not a "fort"; an official fort is the headquarters of a regiment. However, it resembles a fort in its construction.

The birdseye view shows the general layout and orientation of Outpost Number Nine; features are explained in the Key.

The detail shows a cross-section through the outpost's double walls, which ingeniously combine the functions of fortification and shelter.

The walls are constructed of sod, dug from the prairie on which Outpost Number Nine stands, and are sturdy enough to withstand an assault by anything less than artillery. The roof is of log beams covered by planking, tarpaper, and a top layer of sod. It also provides a parapet from which the outpost's defenders can fire down on an attacking force.

one ————————————

It was the summer of 1855 along the banks of the upper Missouri. It was a hot but dry day, not unpleasant, and the songs of birds were in the air. But Second Lieutenant Warner Conway, sitting astride his army mount, was oblivious to such niceties. Rather, he was appalled by what he saw.

Spread out before him was a scene such as he'd heard about but never seen. Native Americans, Indians, dead or dying without a blow from the white man having been struck. Devastated by fever, they lay about, plagued by chills, dreadful aches, and finally rashes that phased into ugly lesions. Mercifully, death soon brought release.

"They have no natural defenses," said Captain Wilbur. "Not against any of our diseases—measles, cholera, scarlet fever, and this, the worst, smallpox."

Lieutenant Conway dismounted and stood beside his bay gelding. He was a young man, tall, rangy, and heavy-boned. He would put on weight over the years, but his frame would carry it easily. He glanced at his captain, who'd remained mounted.

1

Captain Wilbur was a short man, heavy-torsoed but short. Conway's eyes, though he stood on the ground, were almost level with those of the mounted captain. It was one reason why Mr. Conway had dismounted; astride his horse, he towered over the captain, and he knew that made Captain Wilbur uncomfortable and testy.

"Isn't there anything they can do?" asked Mr. Conway.

"There's nothing *anyone* can do, once they get it," said Wilbur. "I hear they can give some kind of shots that might prevent it, but . . ."

Conway eyed the shallow craters on Captain Wilbur's face. He'd wondered about them.

"Yes, Mr. Conway, I've had the damn disease. That's what caused these things you're looking at."

"Sir! I wasn't looking at—"

"Yes you were, Conway, but I don't mind. In Europe, back in the last century, everyone was supposed to have had it at one time or another. But you haven't, have you?"

"No, sir!"

"Then you just stay where you are. Matter of fact, if the wind starts blowing our way, you take off. You hear me? That's an order."

"Yes, sir!"

"That's how it gets passed. Contact, or someone breathes it out into the air and someone else breathes it in. It doesn't live long in the air, but then it doesn't take long to get from that camp to here, given a brisk wind."

Conway started paying very close attention to the prevailing air currents.

"*I* can't get it anymore, y'see," the captain went on, "because I already had it. At least that's what those bastards in the Sanitary Corps say. They'd better be right."

They'd ridden out of Fort Leavenworth—Captain Wilbur, Mister Conway, and a platoon of mounted infantry, and followed the Missouri north and northwest. Along the way they'd encountered a few sites where tipi poles still stood and human bones lay scattered about, obviously the ruins of Indian camps.

"They had the right idea," the captain had said. "Didn't help, but it was the right idea."

"I don't understand, sir," Warner Conway had said.

The captain hadn't explained then, but he did now. "As I said, there's nothing to be done except isolate the sick ones and stay the hell away. There may have been some healthy ones left in this village, but they're long gone, leaving these to die. A week, a month, a year from now, this village will look like those we passed. Tipis collapsed and rotting, bones picked clean. But the ones that got away, they may be sick anyway—takes a while to show up—and may be passing it on to someone else right now." He shook his head. "You know, Lieutenant, some say that before we'd seen or shot a single goddamn Indian, any of these Plains Indians anyway, we'd already killed about half of them."

Conway frowned, and Wilbur continued, "Sure. The white man, the Spaniards, they brought all these diseases with them, starting with Columbus. Smallpox, measles, about any you can think of. And the story goes that about fifty years ago, some war party into New Mexico—Pawnee, I think—brought smallpox back up to the lower Platte. Spread from there down to Texas, cutting a swath. Then, about fifteen, twenty years ago, there was another big smallpox epidemic, north of here but right along this Missouri. Brought by steamboat passengers, best guess. Slowly spread farther on up the Missouri. Cut some tribes in half. Damn near wiped out the Mandan and Assiniboine. Mandan were farming tribes, didn't have anywhere to run or any way to get there. Crow, Blackfoot, they all nearly got cut in half. And that was before we started shooting them. I'll tell you, if it weren't for those diseases, we'd have our hands full, clearing out these red bastards."

Conway, recently out of West Point, wasn't sure that "clearing out these red bastards" was official United States government policy, or the right idea, but . . . "What about the Indian medicine I hear talk about, sir?"

"Not worth a hoot in hell, Lieutenant. A lot of mumbo-jumbo that doesn't add up to much. Keeps them busy, keeps them fooled, keeps them happy sometimes, but that's about it. 'Course, having a happy, satisfied mind will sometimes cure what ails you, you know that. You get way down in the dumps and your body starts feeling bad. But they've got this idea that everything's caused by evil spirits that have entered the body, and the way to get better is to wash the evil spirits out. That's why they have all those sweat boxes. And sometimes sweating *is* good too, like if you've got a runny nose or something. But listen to this. They had another big epidemic a while back, again thanks to us—cholera."

Conway frowned, thinking he recalled something. . . .

"You know what the symptoms of cholera are?" the captain asked. "What shows you're sick with it? Vomiting, diarrhea, liquid pouring out of the body. You damn near dry up and blow away. The way to treat it is to pour liquids in, not take them out. But what does the Indian do? Sticks a man with cholera in a sweat box. Thinks it's *good* if he's vomiting—that means the evil spirits are being expelled." The captain shook his head.

"So all these people will just die," said Lieutenant Conway, "and go off to the Happy Hunting Ground."

Captain Wilbur snorted. "Only if the Jesuits have gotten hold of them. Or the Methodists. The Methodists have been out here working their butts off, trying to convert these heathen. The Happy Hunting Ground is just the Indian version of the Christian heaven. Most Indians have some idea or other about what happens after death, but it rarely has anything to do with heaven or hell." Captain Wilbur laughed. "Heaven and hell are for *us*, Mr. Conway. There aren't going to be any Indians there. No niggers, either."

Conway frowned. Captain Wilbur glanced at him suspiciously.

"You're not one of those abolitionists, are you, Conway?"

"No, sir," Conway replied judiciously, "but there seem to be an awful lot of them without me."

"Abolitionists? Or niggers?" Wilbur grinned. "They're already having arguments right there at the fort. There's a bunch that says that slaves ought not be allowed into Kansas. Hell, I don't see why not. Half the states have them, why not all? But I'll tell you, Conway, this here's '55, we've got an election next year, and the next four or five years will tell the story. If things continue the way they are, I figure that in another ten years you'll see this whole damn country divided up into two separate countries, and nobody's going to be able to stop it."

"Are you thinking of a war, sir?"

"A war? Not a chance. Americans killing Americans over slaves? Over niggers? Not a chance. No, if it happens, it'll be peaceful. Tell you what, though. As long as we've got nigger slaves, we might as well have Indian slaves too."

"But this is their land, sir."

Wilbur smiled coldly. "It *was* their land. No more."

Conway's eyes suddenly widened and he stiffened. They were looking down from near the crest of a bluff, and suddenly

4

rising up before them, not twenty yards away, was a tall figure shrouded in black—a dark, spectral presence.

He stood still, staring at them, a tall Indian. His head was covered with a cowl and his eyes were in deep shadow, yet they were clearly visible, seeming almost to glow.

Conway's blood went cold.

The Indian's mouth opened and closed twice, without uttering a sound.

"Like a fish," muttered Captain Wilbur. "He's trying to breathe."

The Indian continued to stare, unblinking.

"Stoic bastards," declared the captain, "and nothing scares them. They . . . they aren't human, it seems. But you'd better get the hell out of here, Lieutenant, especially if he gets any closer."

Lieutenant Conway thought of Flora, his new bride, a delicate flower plucked from Maryland's fertile fields. A fine thing it would be to carry plague back to her warm bed.

"Funny thing is," said Wilbur, "can't say these Indians haven't had their revenge."

"How's that, sir?" asked Conway, keeping his eye on the Indian.

"Well, just about the time we were shipping them smallpox and measles and God knows what else, they were sending us the so-called French disease by return ship."

"The French disease? Do you mean syphilis, sir? Isn't that . . . well, *French*?"

"It is now. And Italian and English and everywhere else, including right back here in America. But the best anyone can figure, it didn't show up until after Columbus and the boys started messing around with those Indians who came to greet them when they landed. The word is that the Indians had it because, being short of women or something, or like any old farmboy, they kept sticking it to their goats or sheep or whatever. Anyway, that's what they got it from, and that's what the Indians gave us in return. Pretty fair exchange, I'd say."

Conway shuddered and remarked carelessly, "I suppose you've had *that* too, sir."

Captain Wilbur glared at him. "I should say not, Lieutenant. And you'd best be careful who you accuse of such foul behavior."

Conway stared at the gaunt, ghostly figure at the edge of the bluff, searching for the eyes that now no longer glowed.

5

"Sorry, sir," Conway said. "I meant nothing by it."

The Indian turned and vanished as quickly as he'd appeared.

The hell he had "meant nothing by it," recalled Captain Warner Conway, commanding officer of Easy Company, a mounted infantry company stationed at Outpost Number Nine, on the High Plains of Wyoming in the year 1877.

It was summer again. Captain Conway stood by the window of the orderly room, staring out over the parade. He had indeed filled out that rangy frame, and now he was not only tall but large. A large, decisive, formidable officer who clearly remembered Captain Wilbur, the officer who had tried to convince him that the Indian could not be reshaped to fit the white man's civilization.

Well, maybe he couldn't, but Captain Wilbur hadn't been much of a help. And if anyone had ever deserved the "French disease," it had been that pint-sized warrior.

The split in the country had come, as Wilbur had predicted, but war had come also, as Wilbur had not foreseen. Wilbur had chosen to fight and die with the Confederacy; Conway had chosen to go with Honest Abe, and had never regretted his choice. And being on the winning side had nothing to do with it. Being on the *right* side was what mattered.

Warner Conway always recalled the story of Lincoln correcting the man who, during the War, had prayed that God was on their side. Lincoln had told him that rather he should pray, or hope, that the Union was on God's side. And that was the way Warner Conway had felt about the War. Win or lose, he'd been on the side he felt he should be on.

But he also respected the beliefs of those who opposed him, the beliefs of men he respected. But Captain Wilbur had not been among them.

He suddenly wondered why he was having these thoughts.

The person standing outside the orderly room, the black-shrouded figure that blocked Captain Conway's clear view of the parade, was what had prompted the grim recollection. It had reminded him of the dying, shrouded Indian who had stood on the bluff overlooking the village and the headwaters of the Missouri, and had marked Conway with his burning, accusing eyes.

This figure turned about abruptly and, seeing Conway through the window, smiled. But his eyes also had a glow, an unworldly gleam, like those of the Indian long ago. Warner Conway walked outside.

"Father McElroy," said Warner Conway.

"McElroy, yes," answered the man, beaming, "but I am not Catholic, Captain."

Warner Conway was not in the best of moods, hadn't been for several months, if not years. And his memory had just reminded him unnecessarily that twenty-two years before he'd been a second lieutenant, that he'd emerged from the Civil War a first lieutenant, and that not too long after that, he'd made captain. But here he was, still a captain. Time, and promotion, had seemed to stand still.

"Then what the hell are you?" demanded Warner Conway.

"Merely a minister of God, a simple man of—"

"That's right, a humble shepherd." Conway took a deep breath of hot, dry air. "What was it—Methodist?"

"Presbyterian." McElroy sighed. "Still Presbyterian."

Conway nodded. "That's right. The Methodists came through last week. And some Jesuits, but they were headed much farther west, Oregon country, if I'm not mistaken."

"There is room for all to do God's work."

Conway nodded again. He couldn't remember the last time he'd been to a church. Then he brightened. "The Whitmans, they were Presbyterians, weren't they?" He watched a shadow fall across McElroy's face. "Yes, I'm sure they were. Hope you plan to do things a little differently than they did." McElroy frowned, and Conway said, "The Whitman massacre? You've never heard that mentioned?"

"We have, Captain Conway," said McElroy heavily. "Many, many times. Marcus and Narcissa Whitman were most dedicated, most zealous, most determined to *force* the heathen down the road to divine grace. Unfortunately, they were also dogmatic and unbending. They had nothing in common with the Indian and there was no rapport, rather the opposite. And it seems a cruel paradox that the one time they were truly trying to help those Cayuse Indians—the measles epidemic?—the Cayuse thought they were trying to poison them with their medicine. Truly ironic that that was what led to the massacre."

"Mmm," agreed Captain Conway, "ironic indeed. The Whitmans, as I understand it, were not just rigid but unpleasant. Do you count many of their kind among your number?"

"I, Captain, am probably the most disagreeable," said McElroy, beaming at him.

"Aha . . . Well, then, when do you plan to leave for the reservation?"

"We are already there. Or rather, members of our mission

7

have already moved among the Indians and are preparing the neophytes for my disagreeable arrival."

Did he ever stop beaming? "The Cheyenne are not the push-overs that the Sioux were," Conway pointed out.

"The Sioux took very readily to the concept of one God," said McElroy, a trace of irritation in his voice. "One single Spirit, the concept of grace, of heaven and hell—"

"The Happy Hunting Ground," Conway interjected.

McElroy grimaced slightly. "Saint Peter guarding the Gate with his bow and arrow."

"An interesting notion. But you misunderstood me. What I meant was that I think you will find the Cheyenne much less amenable to conversion."

"In our hands, perhaps," allowed the Reverend McElroy, "but not in God's hands. Whomsoever He shall wish to convert, He shall convert."

"The Cheyenne are kind of old-fashioned."

"So was Mary Magdalene, from the oldest of fashions, harlotry."

Captain Conway's jaws clamped shut. He'd never won a religious debate, and he was now old enough to know better than to try. He turned to reenter the orderly room, muttering, "Go with God, Father."

"Thank you, Captain," said McElroy.

In the orderly room, Corporal Four Eyes Bradshaw, the bespectacled company clerk, was eyeing the telegraph equipment suspiciously; it had just made a brief, mysterious noise.

"I think there are men out working on the lines, Corporal," said Captain Conway.

First Sergeant Ben Cohen looked up from his daily strength reports. "That's probably Merkin, from Olsen's platoon. Private Merkin thinks he knows something about telegraphs, about 'lectricity."

"Evidently he does," Conway commented.

The captain stepped to the door of the company adjutant's office. The adjutant, First Lieutenant Matt Kincaid, stood quickly behind his desk, folding his pocket knife and putting it hastily in his trouser pocket, then snapping a salute while brushing a small pile of wood shavings off his desk with his other hand. This series of motions was not lost on Captain Conway as he returned the salute of his second-in-command; he knew that Kincaid was wont to carve up his pine desk whenever time lay heavy on his hands, a habit doubtless left over from his school days. Indeed, the desk appeared to Conway to have become smaller recently, the wooden victim of long sieges of boredom. Conway figured it was a relatively harmless habit, so he never commented on it.

"Apparently those missionaries have already begun converting Mr. Lo," he said. "Has anyone talked to the agent?"

"Mallory?" Kincaid said. "I did. I rode over the other day and tried to discourage the whole thing."

Conway genuinely liked Kincaid, in whom he saw something of himself as he had been some ten years ago. They were almost the same height, though Kincaid was somewhat slighter of build, a lanky, rawboned man with a sort of rugged handsomeness about him that, in a more civilized and cosmopolitan setting, would turn the heads of many a comely young woman.

Kincaid continued, "I told Mallory the Cheyenne weren't going to swallow all that God and heaven and hell dung."

"Dung?" wondered Captain Conway, smiling thinly.

"According to the Cheyenne it is. I argued with him for hours. Lot of good it did. As you well know, the Bureau of Indian Affairs thinks the War Department speaks with a forked tongue. But besides that, you might have noticed that one or two of these Presby missionaries are female, and one in particular has got Mallory reciting the Bible backwards and forwards."

Captain Conway nodded understandingly. "But that's still not going to help McElroy and his friends get through to Mr. Lo."

Matt said, grinning, "Yessir, but I suspect Mallory's interests lie—or *lay*—elsewhere."

Unfortunately, Mallory's pursuit of his interests was not working out. The object of the Agent's affections, Miss Amy Selby, was proving admirably devoted to her mission and resolutely chaste. Her fawnlike eyes might moisten and gleam at the thought of an umbaptized Cheyenne babe, but let Bob Mallory gently finger her fall of cornsilk hair and whisper suggestions—rather tame ones, too—into that delicate pink bud of an ear, and those soft wet eyes would freeze over. As a result, Mallory was passing many a troubled night.

"There is but *one* God," thundered a voice through the windows of his agency. Mallory glanced out crossly. What troublemaker was this? The BIA could feed them, clothe them, house them, and properly educate their children, but tamper

9

with their religion? *That* was asking for trouble. But hell, what could he expect from missionaries?

"*You* claim that this is not so," the voice went on, blasting Mallory's uneasy peace of mind, and he went outside to bear witness (to a slaughter, he privately hoped).

The speaker was black-robed, as usual, but pink-complected, with a great bonnet of curly orange hair. "You *do* say there is a principal god who lives above, but then there is also a benevolent god who lives beneath the ground, who has similar powers, and besides *them*, there are the four great spirits that dwell at the four points of the compass. Surely the great Cheyenne have little need for so many spirits, so many demons. They only serve to confuse."

The speaker, one Reverend Pilcher, eyed his congregation, as unfriendly looking a group as he'd ever seen.

"No," he continued resolutely, "there is but one God, Our Father, who lives above us, in heaven, or, as your friends the Sioux have come to believe, the Happy Hunting Ground."

Eyes hardened in the congregation as they recognized the reference to what they regarded as the dim-witted Sioux. Friends, perhaps, but simple and gullible.

"And there are no powers from the four winds, but there *is* a power, an evil power, that lives deep beneath the ground in a place called hell. He too is powerful, but his power is bad, he works to destroy, to make you suffer. And when you die, if you are not loved by God in heaven, and taken to His bosom, Satan, in hell, will gather you and take you below to never-ending pain.

"But listen! Your god Heammawihio—*hē′ ămmă* does mean 'above,' and *wī′ hio* does mean 'chief.' But *wī′ hio* also means 'spider,' and it *also* means 'white man'"—he raised his hands, turning his pink palms out, and puffed out his pink cheeks, as if to emphasize his whiteness—"and it also means mentality of a higher order.

"You know the white man is of superior intelligence. We know things of which you know not. We have instruments of magical power and force. And we tell you that these things are all ours as a gift from the *one God*...and they can be *yours* when you accept that one God, when you *believe*...."

The Reverend Pilcher paused, sweating. It was damned hot. Why couldn't they have gone on a mission to a more northern tribe of heathen?

He saw Mallory grinning at him. He saw him raise his fist

and call out, "Give 'em hell, preacher."

Pilcher once again looked over his congregation, largely breechclouted, though some wore ill-fitting cotton shirts and trousers. A truly stone-faced group.

He noticed one Cheyenne standing apart from the rest. This man, or at least as much of his skin as was showing, appeared to be painted red. And his leggings and shirt looked as if they might have been fashioned from old lodge-skins. He held in the crook of his left arm something that looked like a combination of bow—strung with two strings—and lance, the complete thing about five feet in length. Near one end was tied the stuffed skin of a red-faced Louisiana tanager, and the rest of the lance was adorned with various mysterious symbols. The Cheyenne now transferred the bow-lance from his left to his right, passing it, however, behind his own back. He glared fiercely at Pilcher for a moment and then, with the same behind-the-back movement, returned the lance to the crook of the left arm. The lance head never touched the ground, never even came close.

Finally, this strange Cheyenne opened his mouth and said, "Let us stay and listen." Whereupon the whole damn bunch got to their feet and walked off.

Pilcher's mouth dropped open, and Mallory grinned at him.

"What in the—" sputtered the Reverend Pilcher. "That is, what in the world was *that*? Who was that . . . *red* man?"

"*That* was a *Hohnuhk'e*."

"A what?"

"It's a word that sort of means doing just the opposite of what is said. We call them, in English, Contraries. And that's what the Cheyenne call 'em too, when they're talkin' English. It means that when one of them wants to say yes, or agree, he says no. Ask a Contrary to go away and he comes nearer. There are about two or three in a tribe. These Contraries are special and are taken seriously. And you better not step in a Contrary's tracks, or let them step in yours, or else you'll go footsore and then lame. Let me tell you, it's bad business messin' with a Contrary."

Pilcher found his voice. "And that was a *weapon* he was carrying?"

"Nope. Oh, they carry it into battle all right, but it's only used to *touch* the enemy, to count coup. You know what that means?"

"It's French for 'blow,' isn't it?"

11

"Well, yeah, but what it means to the Indian is just touching the enemy. Don't even have to kill him, just touch, with something you're holding in your hand."

Pilcher was already confused, and Mallory explained, "Look. Say there's a fight. One brave rushes the enemy with . . . hell, he could be holding a goddamn *twig*. But he just touches the enemy with that twig and yells, 'I'm first.' Then another Indian touches the same enemy and yells, 'I'm second.' And so forth. Only three count as honors, but in a big battle it's hard keepin' track. An Indian sees someone lying there, could be dead already, but he touches him, or probably fetches him a full-fledged whack with his battle-axe, and yells, 'I'm second' or whatever. Probably accounts for the fact that after some of these battles the dead look like they've been chopped up a wee bit more than necessary. Probably just some brave trotting along, one after another, whacking away and counting coups. Get it?"

Pilcher had, but wished he hadn't. These Cheyenne obviously had rites and symbols sufficiently complex as to make Christianity seem like child's play. Conversion was clearly going to be a long, tough haul.

"But what does the Bureau of Indian Affairs intend to do about those . . . barbarisms?" Pilcher asked, plainly outraged.

"Nothing, I hope," said Mallory, "if they got any sense. We'll feed 'em, clothe 'em, give 'em shelter, school their kids, but I hope no one in the bureau's planning to mess with their religion. *You* can, but—"

"There was no trouble with the Sioux."

"These ain't Sioux, preacher. The Cheyenne and Sioux are friends, all right, but the way you and me are friends. I ain't about to become a Presbyterian and you ain't about to become a Lutheran."

Pilcher stared at him for a while. "You're *Lutheran*? Why? Have you really ever thought about it?"

"Oh, for cryin' out loud." Mallory shook his head, grinning. Then he got serious. "Hey, look, preacher, you know where Miss Selby's hiding herself? I ain't seen her all day."

"I believe she went off to try to baptize a newborn babe."

Mallory nodded grimly. "*That'll* put her in a good mood," he said.

Crying Eagle, Yellow Bead, and White Bull met in the shadow of a sod hut. The hut had been built for the Cheyenne by the

BIA, but the Cheyenne preferred to live in their tipis. All their robes, blankets, and skins were cut with the circular, conical tipi in mind. The tribal council sat in a circle, braves danced in circles, the sun, moon, and stars swept across the heavens in great arcs. The flat planes and squared corners of the Americans' huts were foreign and unsuitable to these young Cheyenne (and many Cheyenne youths), as was the full range of American life and customs.

"Have you watched the elders," asked Crying Eagle, "when the Black Robes speak? They sit with their mouths open and they nod. When the Black Robes say the earth god is evil, they nod. When the Black Robes say there are no other gods but the Black Robe god, they nod."

"They are only trying to please," suggested Yellow Bead. "The agent has let the Black Robes come among us. If the Black Robes leave unhappy, the agent will be mad and we will eat less, have less to wear."

"That would be bad," said Crying Eagle. "Then we would have to kill him and take what is ours."

"But the elders say we should keep the peace," said White Bull. "And the elders are wise."

"Wise? Look at us. We have no guns, no horses, no freedom. That is wise? A *child* could have led us to this reservation and stripped us of our manhood."

"Ah, Crying Eagle, you are too suspicious, and too warlike. This life is not bad. It is easy. The women do not have to work so hard—"

"Because the agent tries to get *us* to do women's work, he tries to turn us into women. But the way the Americans do this evil thing is guileful like the snake, like—"

"Speak clearly, Crying Eagle," said White Bull.

"It *is* clear. The agent and the Black Robes tell us we can only have one wife. Well, what single woman can do all the things that must be done for a warrior—clean his clothes, raise his children, cook his food? And when one wife is running blood, as they do with each moon, where can the healthy warrior turn if he has no other wives? He must go to another woman—to a relative or to another man's wife—and that will bring shame."

"Yes, that is so. We must have two wives, at least."

Yellow Bead and White Bull nodded, and Crying Eagle despaired; two wives were all it would take to make them happy. "But do you not understand," Crying Eagle pressed them, "how the American is planning to destroy us? Do you not remember stories of how they brought the great sickness and many of our people died? Half were left to rot and be blown across the plains. Now they say they are trying to save us. The Black Robes are going to save us. Ha! Are we, my brothers, to believe them? *Can* we believe them?"

White Bull and Yellow Bead frowned. "It is many a moon since we wore the blue paint," said White Bull, "but I have kept some."

"I too," said Yellow Bead, showing some eagerness.

"Good," said Crying Eagle. "Good. We are ready. The elders' medicine is weak. To have brought us from the triumph at the Greasy Grass to this poor place is to lose much medicine. If they do not show more wisdom, if their medicine proves weak . . ."

"How goes it, Reverend Pilcher?" asked another missionary.

"Not well. They are fearful and superstitious in very strange ways." He wondered if he could get the concept of Contrariness across to this brother. "And they remember the days when white men brought pestilence among them, and they are wary."

"We shall overcome their resistance, though."

"Amen. But I do wish it weren't quite so hot."

two

A small wagon train moved slowly over the Nebraska plains into Wyoming. Eight wagons loaded with forty people and packed with furniture and fittings for their new home . . . wherever that home might be.

The forty people were all members of a fundamentalist religious sect that had been founded by an ancestor of the wagon train's leader and master, Hiram McClellan. It was his family that had, at the turn of the century, discovered the small, fertile valley hidden in the Pennsylvania hills, his family that had revealed the land to a chosen handful of like-minded, Anglo-Saxon immigrants, who had then proceeded to pass the subsequent years in isolation and almost total self-sufficiency. Children were born and raised who never knew a different life existed, who never saw coin or currency, knowing only of their existence through Biblical stories.

Over the years they saw few outsiders. Strangers were kept away or, if they couldn't be kept away, killed. *Sacrificed.*

Theocracy was clearly God's chosen form of government, and it was the way they governed themselves, the most divinely

15

inspired (and probably the maddest) among them chosen as their leader, a position he held for life.

None but members of the McClellan family had held that position, but each succeeding leader seemed a bit more fanatic than his predecessor. Jonathan McClellan, the discoverer of the valley and the founder, had been the first. He'd died at eighty-five and been succeeded by his sixty-five-year-old son, Marcellus, who had died at seventy-nine, to be followed by John and then by Matthew. Which brought them up to 1863, when Matthew, at the age of forty-nine, stood atop a hill and took a Union musket ball between his eyes. The people of the valley had always favored black or gray for clothing and Matthew's gray coat had drawn the fire of an overeager Union private.

For a few days it appeared the valley might be overrun first by Confederate forces and then by Union troops. But it wasn't, and the peace was maintained.

Their isolation had begun to erode with the death of Matthew, however, and with the incursion of outsiders, even if only in the form of a musket ball. And by the time Hiram McClellan, given conditional control of the sect at twenty-five, took full command, fourteen years later, the signs of the times had been read clearly. And, Hiram further suspected, their theocracy would not stand up to the light of civilization. Their valley would be discovered and invaded, and their ways changed.

So Hiram gathered his flock and they set out westward to discover a new hiding place, a new home. The route they followed led straight across the continent to Wyoming's South Pass over the Rockies. Unless, of course, they swung north at some point to follow the migration to Oregon. But only Hiram knew their goal, only he even knew there was a continent out there to be crossed.

So far, they'd driven unswervingly west, staying off main roads and avoiding settlements, towns, and cities. They'd moved slowly, having to stop often to let their horses and cows graze, since they carried no feed, but they'd moved steadily. Only once had they come in contact with strangers. One wagon wheel had come apart in Iowa. They'd replaced it, but yet another had broken while they were passing near to the Nebraska town of Schuyler, a town situated in the eastern part of the state, on the Union Pacific Line, and not far from the Platte River.

Three men had gone to town, Hiram and two others. They'd

stayed in the smithy, eyes fixed on the blacksmith and their wheels as he worked on them. But a number of townspeople happened by, casting looks at the funereal gray-and-black garb of Hiram and his companions, and the wagoneers did have occasion to dip a cup into the communal barrel of drinking water.

The work done, the wagon train moved on.

Ten days later the wagon train drew abreast of the town of North Platte, where the north fork of the Platte River came down from the northwest to join the somewhat larger south fork, which combination then flowed east as the Platte River. At that point, several members of the wagon train began to get sick. They ran fevers, their eyes were red and watery, their heads congested, and there was profuse nasal discharge.

Hiram McClellan was outraged. Seldom had a single one of his people suffered a single day of illness. They hardly knew what illness was. Hiram was sure that evil spirits had invaded his vulnerable companions during their short stay in Schuyler. The only answer was prayer, to drive the evil spirits away.

However, Hiram McClellan's prayers were to prove as ineffective as the Indians' medicine, gods, herbs, and prayers, when it came to dealing with an outbreak of measles. Especially since the sect's years of isolation had left them just as vulnerable as the Indians to new disease.

And as the wagon train continued west, following a trail equidistant between the Union Pacific Line to the south and the north fork of the Platte River to the north, moving on across the border into Wyoming, the measles spread through the wagon train and worsened.

"Perhaps we need a doctor," ventured an elder who somehow had learned more than he should have.

"What is a doctor?" asked another, suitably ignorant.

Hiram declined to debate the need for, or even define the function of, a doctor. "A doctor," he roared rhetorically, "can do more than *God*?!"

Some hundred miles west of them, beyond Wyoming's Black Hills (a lower extension of the Black Hills so beloved of the Dakota tribes and later to be renamed the Laramie Mountains) other, if dissimilar, requests of the Almighty were being made.

"Please, God," asked the widow Bennett of a cross on her bedroom wall, "is Jeffrey Dow the proper man for Naomi and myself?"

17

The widow Bennett, who neither expected nor got an immediate reply, was the widow of Arnold Bennett, who'd died two years previously, his spleen ruptured by the kick of a draft horse.

He, his wife, and his daughter had staked claim to and proven out a quarter section halfway between Easy Company's Outpost Nine and a town that lay some forty miles to the east of the post. They'd staked the claim in 1870, making improvements and paying taxes on the land for the next five years, at which point they received clear title to the 160 acres. Then Arnold died. And although, in 1877, the widow Bennett could not vote, she could own property and was legally considered the head of the family.

But she didn't want that position. She wanted a man, a strong, healthy man to serve her needs, her wants, run the farm, and be a father to Naomi, to say nothing of fathering more offspring. She wanted to be a wife and mother. But was Jeff Dow the right candidate?

She thought he loved her, *liked* her anyway, and liked Naomi, and knew farming because he'd grown up farming. And he was a good-looking man. She was older than he was, but he didn't know how much older and she'd never tell him. And as she stayed well out of the sun, often employing sunbonnets the size of parasols, her complexion did not reveal her thirty-one years. *And*, most important of all considerations, Jeffrey Dow, an Army of the West private stationed with Easy Company at Outpost Number Nine, was due to be discharged within a few days, and was therefore available, a prime candidate.

But there were times when his mind and mouth disturbed her, suggesting shortcomings in seriousness and sensitivity—in her opinion, anyway.

But then, Arnold Bennett had been as sensitive as a wagon wheel. It was a wonder that the horse that kicked him hadn't broken its hoof.

The widow Bennett's sod house, barn, barnyard, outhouse, chicken house, hogpen, and garden were located at the northwest corner of the quarter section, with the house and barn facing south. They took up about three of the 160 acres. The rest of the land was divided into four approximately equal forty-acre plots. Arnold Bennett had been a proper and industrious, if untalented, farmer, and had taken care to let one or two fields lie fallow each year. This year just one had been left fallow.

Of the other three, one had been planted partly with oats, partly with barley. Another had been planted with a new kind of wheat, red wheat, stuff from Russia that some people called Mennonites had brought with them. It was supposed to grow well in hard climates. The third was planted with corn. Jeff Dow was going to have to do something about that. Any Western farmer, and Dow had talked to some, knew that corn didn't do well at that altitude. He'd have to tell the widow that, impress her with his knowledge. Then she'd have to thank him—send Naomi off to do some chore and climb into the sack with him. Yes indeed. Oh, thank you, Jeff, thank you. . . .

Jeff Dow was wandering along behind the team of horses, turning over the field that was lying fallow. It probably didn't need turning over, but if it wasn't that, he'd probably be cleaning the hen house out, and he'd had enough chicken shit for that week.

He looked over at the field of corn. It was growing hardly at all, despite the presence of Mr. Arnold "Horse's Ass" Bennett.

The presence he referred to was that of a scarecrow, propped up at the eastern end of the cornfield and grimly attired in the late Mr. Bennett's black Sunday suit. "Might keep the devil away," Dow muttered, "but them black ol' crows prob'ly think he's their daddy." Dow shook his head, smiling, then looked behind to examine the crooked furrow he'd plowed. "Better keep my mind on business," he mumbled, "else Zelly's gonna think I ain't such a great farmer."

Zelly was his nickname for the widow Bennett, Giselle Bennett. He thought about her, about her soft, willing body. She sure didn't look thirty-one, didn't act it either, and would probably die if he told her he knew her age.

Giselle had tried to claim she'd been a child bride, but Naomi knew her mother had been about eighteen when she got hitched, and nineteen when she birthed Naomi, and she'd told Jeff as much. Jeff had a weathered look, and Naomi'd thought he might admire an older woman like her mother.

Ha! But hell, she was better looking still than any gal he'd ever had, and she owned the house and land outright (and he knew she had some money stashed away in the town bank too), and she wanted a man so badly he could marry her and still do about anything he wanted. And Naomi was pretty near a woman herself.

He scratched his head, shoving back the blue forage cap.

19

Sure was nice of the first sergeant to let him have all this time off. Sergeant Cohen knew what was going on, but he was a strange one. Kept after Dow to reenlist, but still gave him all the time he wanted to get to know the widow real well. Maybe Cohen knew something he didn't know, or figured he'd screw up.

He glanced up again at the scarecrow . . . and saw two, three, then *four* scarecrows! And they were *moving*!

Then he realized that it was a group of riders—ten, twelve, maybe—circling around the plowed and planted fields. The riders saw Dow, and one raised a hand and Dow halted his team and strode to meet them.

They were an exceedingly scroungy-looking group. It wasn't their clothes, which were dark and drab and almost sinister, as much as their faces, their expressions, the way they sat astride their horses, as if certain positions caused pain.

"Howdy," cried Dow, drawing close.

"Howdy yerself," said the man who appeared to be the leader. "'Less'n yer borryin' them clothes an' th' cap, I'd judge you t' be a sojer." He swept his hat off and brushed at flies that were bothering his horse.

"You'd be judgin' right," confirmed Dow. Standing close now, he saw that the man's scalp appeared kind of moth-eaten, with hair missing in clumps. Hardly better than the grimy gray hat he was waving. And his eyes were red and inflamed. And though the man appeared lanky, his arms and hands and even his neck seemed kind of swollen. And as far as Dow could tell with a quick glance—he didn't want to look like he was staring—the rest of the group didn't look much better.

"Are we headed right for Outpost Number Nine?"

Dow was tempted to send them off in some other direction, but said instead, "Yeah, yer headin' right, 'bout another twenny miles thataway."

The leader nodded absently and urged his horse on. The rest trailed after him, saying nothing. Polite bastards, thought Dow. Then he caught the eye of one of three women who brought up the rear. They didn't look too healthy either, but they sure weren't bad looking. And the one whose eye he'd caught . . .

The group of twelve rode on steadily. Twenty miles. Two or three more hours of easy riding.

But not easy enough for Amos Fletcher, the leader. He

20

wasn't feeling good, but then he hadn't felt good for a long time, not for months, not since he'd picked up whatever it was he had, which was the same thing the rest of them had. Rashes, sores. They'd gone away after the first few weeks, but now they were back. But they weren't so bad. It was the *other* stuff—the headaches, sore joints, sore throats, hair loss. They didn't get the real bad sores again, but God only knew what they had. It sure wasn't fun, and he wished it would go away.

Fletcher thought back to the previous evening, when he'd met his brother at the fort that was the regimental headquarters for this region. His brother, who figured he was better than the rest of the family. He was a soldier, he'd said, real proudly. But a *clerk* was all he really was.

"Don't get near me! Don't touch me!" his brother had screamed.

Fletcher'd scared his miserable brother half to death. Didn't loving brothers hug each other?

Fletcher hadn't seen his brother, who'd changed his name to Morgan, in nearly five years. While Morgan had slipped off and joined the army, Fletcher'd gone a different route, gathered a gang, and terrorized eastern Kansas and Nebraska and parts of Iowa and Missouri. Quantrill reborn.

But then it had gotten a little hot for them, a little tight, and they'd already picked up the sickness, whatever it was that was bothering them. They'd made that last killing in Missouri . . . and that had been fun, dammit, that had been *fun*.

Fletcher smiled, remembering the large farm, the family, the women. Young women, some really young. They'd killed the menfolk, and then had their way with the women. The older ones they'd had to kill afterwards, but the young ones, the girls, no more than kids, really, that had been as close to heaven as he ever expected to get.

Left those girls lying out there, near dead, let the hogs out to snort and nose around them.

Jesus, that'd been fine. Pickett had been their names. John Pickett and family, of Pickett's Landing.

He'd wondered if they'd been related somehow to the Civil War Pickett. He'd hoped so. A fine way to get back at those bastards, even this long after the War.

Pickett. A lot of Picketts wandering around the Western territories. Lot of John Picketts too, including one well-known bounty hunter. It'd be a laugh if he'd been related.

But that had been their last big action. Fletcher had decided

21

it was time to head west, for Oregon and thereabouts. There'd be a whole slew of new and easy pickings there. But they'd kind of like a good stake before heading over the mountains. And that was where Fletcher's loving brother, John Morgan, came in.

"Now when does the payroll get in?"

"Any time," his brother had replied. "They seem a mite casual about that, but there ain't no chance of you gettin' that. They keep it in a safe. And this is an army base, for Chrissakes. They'd shoot the hell out of you."

"But they got to send it from here to the other outposts, right? And they won't send no platoon along with it, right? Just a small patrol, right? Now where's this Easy Company located?"

Corporal John Morgan told him.

"Now listen. We're goin' over to Easy, hang around there. We'll tell them we're waiting for word to head south to meet— hell, I don't know, some wagon train to New Mexico, something like that—but when the paymaster leaves here for Easy with the payroll, you send me a wire, saying something, *anything*, and we'll know they're on the way. And remember, my name over there'll be Cranmore. That's Cranmore—got it? We'll ride out and take care of them, and while the soldiers ride south, thinkin' they're chasin' us, we'll be ridin' like hell for Oregon with a bundle of money."

"I don't know," said Morgan dubiously.

"Yes you do, *brother*. You don't want us hangin' around here, do you? Lettin' on that Corporal John Morgan is really related to the notorious Fletcher gang? The flyers may not have gotten this far west yet, but they will. So we don't have much time, and neither do you. . . ."

Fletcher remembered the look on his brother's face. He also remembered his brother's last words. "You'd better get that stuff looked at. Find a doctor, maybe he'll know what it is."

They had found doctors, demanded diagnosis under threat of death. And they had killed half the doctors they'd seen. But none had come up with an accurate diagnosis or remedy. Or, if they had, they'd been afraid to say it, afraid to identify the disease.

The trouble may have been that the disease they suffered from was often called "the great imitator." There were at least forty diseases that the skin rashes and lesions resembled; twenty-three that the mouth lesions resembled; at least sixteen diseases that the genital lesions resembled. No wonder the various doctors, under the stress of a death threat, misdiagnosed their ailment.

But what they all had, in the latter part of its secondary phase, was syphilis.

Thus they were probably doomed, sooner or later, but they were blissfully unaware of that fact, and for them and for those they met, the only question was how many innocents would they hurt or destroy before that doom caught up to them?

Then again, they were the type that, had they known the nature of their disease, probably would have enjoyed spreading it around.

Which sounds insane, but as they'd ridden out of sight, John Morgan had breathed a sigh of relief and muttered, "They're crazy. They're *crazy*."

The rider had not quite topped the rise when he heard the yipping and whooping. And then the sound of gunfire.

When he did reach the top he saw a wagon, an army ambulance, trying to outrun four Indians.

Probably Cheyenne, thought the rider, but maybe not. The way the Army of the West was pushing the red man all over the landscape, it could be any tribe. Sioux, Arapaho, maybe even Crow.

The race was a good one. The ambulance was drawn by a team of four army horses, big, strong, and possessing greater endurance than the Indian ponies. But the Indian ponies were faster over the short haul and might catch the ambulance before it could get away.

The rider was tempted to just sit on the brow of the hill and watch, as if at a horse race, pretty certain the ambulance would make its escape. But he was not even certain that he cared if it did, such was his state of mind.

There were obviously armed men aboard the ambulance; someone was firing a gun.

But then he saw, as the race crossed before him, from right to left, that the Indians were drawing close. Maybe the Indians themselves had some army horses. That'd change things a lot.

Damn. He *did* care. Abruptly, he kicked his horse into motion and charged down the hill, loosening his Colts in their holsters as he did so. As he closed the distance, he spied the blue warpaint. Cheyenne.

The Cheyenne, for their part, were shooting what sounded

23

like repeaters, but not with great effect. They were not actually, at that moment, on a killing raid. They'd been looking for stray Crow or Arapaho or, best of all, the hated Pawnee—whom they would have killed or died trying. But they hadn't found any, just the wagon with the Americans, on whom they decided to count coup. Not that they intended to kill and scalp, rather just get close enough to *touch*. Of course, even being touched with a hatchet was hardly a pleasant experience; in fact such a touch could easily kill. But in any case, their shooting was more for show and to cause fear than for lethal effect. And to wound and slow one or more of the four-horse team would make their coup-counting easier.

Occupying the wagon, their hearts in their throats, were four people. Privates Bielkiewicz and Vaughn from the 1st Squad of Lieutenant Smaldoon's Second Platoon, Amy Breckenridge, the platoon sergeant's wife, and Cassie Smaldoon, the platoon leader's sister.

Cassandra Smaldoon, a pretty, pert blond in her mid-twenties, had come west to join her officer-brother and find for herself an officer-husband. But, having found the pickings slim, she was now a quiet realist, still pretty but no joy to be around. And she'd finally gotten bored of looking at the same four outpost walls every day of the week. She'd talked Amy Breckenridge into joining her, talked her brother into assigning a wagon or carriage and two escorts, and off they'd gone to see the countryside. There'd been no hostile activity of late, and it had been thought safe.

And they had seen the countryside, which rapidly became boring. Rolling prairie. Rolling, rolling, rolling.

"A sea of grass the color of a lion's mane," said Private Bielkiewicz, and both Cassie and Amy stared at him. Bielkiewicz was no bargain, as far as brains *or* beauty were concerned.

"Where'd you hear *that*?" demanded Amy Breckenridge.

"Heard Lieutenant Kincaid call it that. Sounds good, don't it? 'Course, I never *seen* a lion. . . ." He laughed. "But I guess I'll know what to look for if I ever do."

"And what's the sky?" asked Amy, eyes narrowing.

Private Vaughn, handling the reins, glanced at the sky and ventured, "Looks blue to me."

"Private Bielkiewicz?" pursued Amy.

Bielkiewicz, appearing embarrassed, muttered, "Cobalt blue."

"Kincaid again?"

"Good Lord, yes, ma'am."

Amy Breckenridge and Cassie Smaldoon exchanged smiles. "There's more to our company adjutant than meets the eye," said Amy.

"Or ear," added Cassie. And that was when the Cheyenne attacked.

Vaughn started whipping the horses while Bielkiewicz set himself up in back with his rifle, the Springfield Trapdoor .45-70, Allin Conversion.

Amy Breckenridge grabbed one of Vaughn's pistols, the Smith & Wesson .45-caliber Schofield model, or "Scoff," and set herself up to do some damage.

Cassie Smaldoon, never having fired a weapon, decided this was a good time to learn. She picked up Vaughn's Springfield and tried to figure it out.

Vaugn screamed back at her that it was a single-shot weapon and needed to be reloaded after every shot. A good man can get off about twenty shots a minute. Cassie got off one.

The Cheyenne were getting closer, and the four-horse team was beginning to slow, when the stranger hit the Cheyenne from the side.

Knowing he could get close unnoticed, the rider had eschewed the rifle hanging in its scabbard and let a brace of Colts do the work. Rising in his stirrups to steady himself, he lay down a thunderous and reasonably effective barrage. One Cheyenne sagged and the rest started pulling their horses up, while the rider rode on after the ambulance.

He soon caught up as the wagon flowed further and then stopped.

The rider had not yet dismounted, and was just beginning to smile down at the women, when he suddenly rose up and then pitched slowly from his saddle.

One of the retreating Cheyenne, annoyed at having his coup-counting thwarted, had paused to send a single shot toward the wagon. As it happened, that particular Cheyenne was carrying a Sharps, courtesy of some dead buffalo hunter, and a .50-caliber slug from it easily covered the distance and crashed into the small of the rider's back, exiting through his belly just above his waistband.

A bad wound, nearly always fatal, but the soldiers and women rallied around.

Cassie and Amy stripped their undergarments off, tore them

25

into strips, and bound the man's midsection tighter than a drum. In the meantime, Vaughn and Bielkiewicz turned the wounded horse loose to wander back to post or die, and hitched the stranger's horse to the rest of the team. Then they loaded the stranger onto the wagon, now truly an ambulance, and lit out for Outpost Number Nine and Easy Company.

three

The eagle-eyed and apprehensive Private Tompkins,
scanning the prairie from his guard post atop the tower over
Outpost Number Nine's main gate, was the first to sight the
charging ambulance. He passed the word to Guard Corporal
Horace Kane, who in turn relayed it to Guard Sergeant Breckenridge, who, knowing his wife was aboard that ambulance,
made things happen. Therefore, by the time the ambulance
came careening through the main gate onto the parade, the
entire post had turned out to see what was up.

Private Vaughn was making his terse report almost before
the ambulance was completely stopped, before Matt Kincaid,
Sergeant Breckenridge, and Lance Corporal Enright had
grabbed hold of the lead horses and practically brought them
to their knees.

"Get a stretcher!" roared Captain Conway. "And Dutch,
wash up and get your tools ready."

Mess Sergeant Dutch Rothausen was, in a pinch, the com-

27

pany surgeon. The closest legitimate army surgeon was at Regimental HQ, and the doctor in town was close enough to help sometimes, but not this time.

Dutch and his assistant surgeons—assistant cooks, actually—gathered all their sharpest knives and dumped them in a boiling pot along with assorted tweezers, clamps, and whatever other tools might be pressed into surgical service.

The wounded man was brought into the mess and laid unconscious on a table. His bandages were soaked deep red.

Dutch and his assistants, Corporal Perkins and Private Washburn (also known as Heartburn, not affectionately), unwrapped the bandages and exposed the gaping exit wound in the lower left abdomen.

"Holy shit," said Dutch. He'd attended Penn State, but had not studied medicine—agriculture, rather—and this lay well beyond his schooling and his practical experience; no man wounded like that had ever reached him alive.

"Shit, he's a goner," said Corporal Perkins, already starting to think of the bread he'd been baking.

"No he's not!" cried Cassie Smaldoon, who'd followed the litter in. "He *can't* be."

"Get me some twine," said Dutch. "We'll tie off whatever's bleeding first . . . if I can *find* the goddamn things."

And so it went for a while, searching for sources of bleeding and tying them off. But finally they were stumped. Obviously they had to reattach the tied-off ends, but such was Dutch's knowledge of the cardiovascular system that he wasn't sure what connected with what. He was apt to join an artery to a vein.

Why didn't the bastard just die, wished Dutch. Save him a hell of a lot of work, to say nothing of embarrassment—everyone was watching him, thinking he was going to perform some miracle.

"Excuse me, Sergeant," said someone, and Dutch was rudely elbowed aside.

The person who had spoken was an army lieutenant, but a stranger to Dutch. He peered into the wound, and then started reaching for knives and needles. "Where are some goddamn needles and thread? Gut! Get me some gut!" he roared.

"Who the hell are you?" growled Dutch, grabbing a rag and using it to sponge up blood inside the wound.

The officer didn't answer, instead bent down close to the wound and poked here and there. "Lucky bastard. Blew everything to pieces except his vitals. He's got a chance ... gotta be made of iron to still be alive . . . might make it. . . ."

Then, in a pause while Corporal Perkins was threading up another string of gut, he turned to Dutch, smiled, and said, "Marlowe. Surgeon General sent me."

In the meantime, other strangers had pushed in around Dutch and his cooks, eventually easing them out of the picture altogether, strangers who showed expertise. Dutch, Perkins, and Washburn were reduced to second-line assistants, which they didn't mind one damn bit. In fact, Dutch got quite a kick out of seeing real artists at work.

But it couldn't go on forever, and didn't. Marlowe finally stepped back and said, "That's all we can do. The rest is up to him. Let him lie here awhile, then move him to some comfortable quarters. I don't guess the men will enjoy chowing down with him lying about."

Marlowe then stepped out of the mess, followed by Dutch and Matt Kincaid, leaving Cassie Smaldoon staring down at the still face of the stranger.

Outside, they stood silent for a while. Finally Dutch said, "Guess you're a real doctor. Where the hell did you come from?"

Marlowe waved toward the main gate, just inside of which were gathered several wagons. "As I said, the U.S. Surgeon General sent us. Sanitary Corps. Here to vaccinate the heathen against smallpox and teach them a few things about personal hygiene."

Matt smiled. "You'd better get a move on if it's heathen you're looking for. The Presbyterians are over there right now, fighting for their eternal souls."

"Are they, now? Those missionaries can sometimes be a real pain in the butt."

"And if you come at them, jabbing those needles, you not only have all their old gods to deal with, but Jesus Christ himself." Matt grinned.

"I was not aware," said Marlowe, "that the New Testament prohibits vaccination."

"Maybe not, but if that'll get the Cheyenne over on the Bible-thumpers' side, then you'd better watch out."

"Cheyenne? Is that who we're dealing with?"

"Didn't you know?"

"When it comes to smallpox, one Indian's the same as another."

29

"The Cheyenne aren't going to be easy. They're a suspicious and feisty bunch."

"'Scuse me, doc," said Dutch, seizing upon a pause in the exchange," but I gotta tell you how I admired your work. I've never seen real surgery like that."

Matt's eyes widened. "You haven't? I thought—"

"Don't hurt to fib, Matt, 'specially when there ain't no one else around. Besides, I'm just talking about that special stuff you just seen. I can cut and cauterize just as good as the next fellow, but . . . tell me, doc, where'd you get your training?"

"Penn State. You've heard of it?"

Dutch Rothausen almost choked.

Lieutenant Marlowe took Dutch's silence for ignorance and started walking toward his wagons and the sutler's store beyond. Matt Kincaid joined him. But they hadn't gone far when Dutch shouted after them, "Hell, I went there."

Marlowe paused and turned, evidently pleased by the news. "We'll talk about it later," he said. "For now, though, keep an eye on the patient." Then he and Matt walked on.

"You're good enough to hang out a shingle," said Matt.

Marlowe nodded without conceit. "Thought I'd get some experience first," he said. "*And* see the frontier. The commission seems to come with the job, but please don't call me 'lieutenant.'" He looked around, having finished with that subject. "This is a *fort*," he said. "I must confess, when they sent us out here I was wondering what an outpost looked like."

"It's a fort, right enough," said Matt, "but you've got to be regimental headquarters or better to be *called* a fort."

"The housing's built right into the walls. Clever."

"And they had to haul the timber a hell of a ways for those walls, but it's true, everything's built right in. The gate faces east, as you can see, which mostly has to do with the sun rising in the east and having your backside to the prevailing winds, which come from the west, and let me tell you, in the winter they are *cold*.

"Next to the gate there, on the left, beneath the tower, that's the guard house. Then comes the mess—you've been there, down at the corner. Then"—turning around as he walked and pointing north—" the enlisted barracks, enlisted dayroom. Then the west wall, that's officers' country—dayroom, mess, quarters. The orderly room faces the gate, then more officers' quarters and dependent housing." He completed a full turn and pointed south, straight ahead. "More dependent housing, stables—the gate leads to the paddock—and then the smithy, storerooms, Skinflint Wilson's supply room—he's ordnance too—then, just before you get to the gate, that's the sutler's. He's civilian, Pop Evans, supplies just about everything that's not issued, and some that is."

"And the guard mount walks along the roofs."

"They're thick, those roofs," Kincaid said. "Timber and sod. But that doesn't mean they don't *leak*. Get a rainy spell, and your bedroom can be ankle-deep in mud."

"Lovely. Well, Lieutenant, I thank you for your tour, even though I will probably never set foot within these confines again."

"Oh?"

"Mmm. After these Cheyenne, it's on north to the Crow."

"Well, the Crow I shouldn't think you'd have any trouble with. Not promising, though."

Marlowe passed him a weak smile. Then he scowled and said, "Good God, who are those people?"

The scroungy gang led by Amos Fletcher had just arrived and had ridden directly to the sutler's, tying up at the hitching rail just out front.

"Plains drifters," muttered Matt. "Scum. There are a lot of 'em floating around the West."

"Who the hell are *they*, Matt?" asked another voice, from behind them.

Matt turned to look at Windy, who'd just come up, silently as usual. "Doctor Marlowe, this is Windy Mandalian, the company's chief scout."

Marlowe regarded Windy frankly. "You look part Indian. Are you?"

Windy only smiled. Rumor had it he was part Cree, to go along with the Armenian and French Canadian he did own up to. "Them folk could do with a bath. They stink worse'n Arnold."

"Arnold's a private," Matt explained, "who regards soap and water as his mortal enemy. Once a month the men have to hogtie and bathe him."

Marlowe was amused only briefly. "It'd take more than a bath to clean *those* men up."

"What do you mean?" asked Matt.

"Truthfully," said Marlowe, "I don't know. Can't even

31

guess. I'd have to do some extensive examining, and there's not the time. In fact, we're supposed to pull out any moment now."

"Better wait for morning," said Matt. "It's a good haul, and you can see if your patient's going to live."

"If he's lived this long, he'll probably make it. Might not wake up for a while, though."

Just then one of the Fletcher gang, a woman, good looking at one time but now made less so by disease, came back out of the sutler's. She looked Matt over appraisingly.

"Looks like you got an admirer," commented Windy.

Matt's eyes went cold. "Not interested."

"And *you'd* better not be, either," Marlowe advised Windy, then said, "Whoops, looks like someone gave the colonel some different advice, Lieutenant. My party's leaving. I'd better hurry or I'll have to walk."

They all said goodbye, and Matt and Windy wandered back over to the mess. They found Captain Conway and First Sergeant Ben Cohen looking down at the unconscious stranger.

Cassie Smaldoon also hovered over him protectively, frequently wiping his brow with a damp rag.

"Who do you suppose he is?" wondered Matt.

"Went through his saddlebags," said Cohen. "Found a lot of flyers, wanted circulars. I'd guess the man's a bounty hunter. Got the guns for it. Funny thing, though. Some of the flyers are dated. Bradshaw checks those things when they come through. He says some of the men on those flyers have been caught or killed."

"Maybe he just didn't know."

"Didn't know or didn't care, like he'd something else on his mind for a while."

"Well," said the captain, "we won't know until he wakes up. *If* he wakes up. The problem is, where'll we put him?"

"We're kind of tight for extra space," said Matt, conscious of Cassie's bright eyes but avoiding them. "Best thing to do, maybe, is stick him into Mr. Smaldoon's quarters, where Cassie can keep an eye on him."

Cassie assumed a superserious, nurselike manner.

"Mr. Smaldoon won't like it," said Ben Cohen, "which is putting it mildly."

"Mr. Smaldoon can bunk with Mr. Fox for a while," said Captain Conway.

Matt grinned. "In which case Mr. Fox"—who was the platoon leader of First Platoon, the one Matt usually rode with—"isn't going to like *that*."

"What've I got," growled Conway, "a bunch of prima donnas?"

"Fact is," continued Matt, "the two of them will go together like oil and water."

"But," said Sergeant Cohen, "if Mr. Lo really is looking for trouble, then neither Fox nor Smaldoon is going to be spending much time here."

"Well," drawled Matt, "I've got an idea from the descriptions that the wagon attack wasn't all that serious. Few bucks kicking up their heels."

"Kicking up their heels!" exclaimed Cassie.

Matt looked at her. "That's right, Miss Smaldoon. A Cheyenne's idea of fun can be a hell of a lot different from ours."

"Well!" declared Cassie. "Say what you want, but I want to take care of this man, and if my brother doesn't like it, to hell with him."

Captain Conway smiled. "That's the spirit, Cassie. I guess it's settled."

The captain couldn't wait to see how Smaldoon took the news. Smaldoon had come up through the ranks, received a battlefield commission, and was a good deal touchier about protocol than the usual military-school product. Rank not only had its privileges; with Lieutenant Smaldoon, it *demanded* its privileges. Being shoved in with the barely competent Lieutenant Maynard Fox should send him up the walls.

Leaving the mess, Captain Conway asked Matt, "Is Fox really as helpless as he seems?"

"No," said Matt. "Just overcautious. Won't make a move until he's sure he knows what he's doing. And so far, being new, he doesn't know much. But give him time."

"As long as we've got time, he'll get it. But this peaceful spell's not going to last."

"I know, sir, I know." Matt grinned. "And I can't wait for it to end."

Captain Conway walked on to the orderly room, and Matt Kincaid went to buy a beer at the sutler's store.

Before he got inside, though, he was intercepted by Amos Fletcher. Matt had to force himself not to leap away from the obviously diseased creature.

"Good day to ya, Lieutenant," said Fletcher. "Whereabouts can we bed down? We're headin' south from here, down south around New Mexico."

Did that call for a comment? After a bit, Matt said, "Yes, you're going south to New Mexico, so?"

"Well . . . we can't leave till we get a wire sayin' the folks we're gonna join up with down south—a wagon train?—that they're gonna be there. So we're waitin' here for the wire. You'll let us know soon it comes in, wontcha? Name's Cranmore."

Matt was nodding impatiently. The man did not sound completely sane.

"*So* . . . we gotta stay somewhere. . . ."

"You can camp just outside of the walls. You'll be safe there unless some hostile really wants to get you, in which case you wouldn't be safe anywhere."

Fletcher nodded dumbly, then said, "What do you fellars do for fun?"

"Fun?" The man was so odious that the concept of *fun* was something Matt had difficulty associating with him. "Fun? Well, there's a town about a half-day's ride east of here. Most of the time, when the men want some fun, that's where they head."

One of the women of Fletcher's gang had wandered up. She grinned at Matt. It was odd how a once reasonably pretty face could achieve such an unpleasant effect. "There ain't nothing else you can think of"—her voice was surprisingly musical—"to do for fun?" There was mischief in her inflamed eyes.

Matt remained wooden-faced, shook his head, and said dully, "Nope, that's about it, what I said. Town. About a half-day's ride." And he turned on his heel and walked away.

34

four _____

Over at the Cheyenne Reservation, the missionaries, including the newly arrived Reverend McElroy, were having a tough time. They were finding the Cheyenne not only hard to convert but damned contentious. They were almost learning more about Cheyenne beliefs than they were teaching the Cheyenne theirs.

Once they'd absorbed the stuff about the principal god, Heammawihio, and his subordinates—East, West, North, South, and Underground—all of whom didn't sound too unusual, they learned about Creation, the Land of the Dead, and several other things.

When it came to Creation, Heammawihio first made people to live, *just* to live. If they died, they would be dead for only four nights and then they'd live again. Heammawihio soon realized, though, that that wasn't going to work. It would make people too brave, lead to too much killing. And that was why he changed his mind and made people die forever.

Heammawihio himself lived for a while with his creations

on earth, but then he went up to live in the sky, and he told his people that when they died they would come and live with him.

That sounded fine to the missionaries. A God above, with a heaven for his chosen people, wouldn't be too hard to deal with in making converts. But then things got a bit trickier.

Seyan was the place where Heammawihio and those who died lived on, excepting only those who had killed themselves. But aside from that particular exception, of which even the Jesuits would have approved, all others, the brave and the cowardly, the good and bad, all went there. All who died were equal. After death there was neither reward for virtue nor punishment for sins. In other words, no Judgment Day.

That, naturally, stuck in the missionaries' throats, but there was more to come.

The dead reached Seyan by following the Hanging Road, or Milky Way. And there they lived as they had lived on earth—hunting, warring, and so forth.

Of course, all of this was oral legend, myth, and common belief; there was nothing written, and there might occur variations. Some believed simply that after death they went to live with the Old Woman, or Grandmother, in her snug lodge in the north, under the Northern Lights, which were the reflections of her medicine fire. These believers were tired of war, of the hunt. They just wanted to sleep and eat—the Old Woman fed those who lived with her forever on the Fat Cow.

Then, returning to the orthodox beliefs, there was *tasoom*, a man's spirit, literally his shade, or shadow. *Tasoom* could be the shadow of any animate thing: man, horse, bird, dog. Those who died became shadows. And if a man saw his shade, or shadow, it was a sign he would soon die. And if a man was dying, and had lost consciousness though he still breathed, they said, "His *tasoom* has been gone a long time; he is only just breathing."

Many Indians refused to be photographed by the occasional early photographer, because they believed that when the picture was taken away, the life of the subject, his *tasoom*, was also taken away, and the subject would soon die.

Similarly, when early visitors, including the missionaries, tried to enchant the Cheyenne with small mirrors, many Cheyenne refused to look into them, fearing they would see their shadows and bad luck would stalk them.

And so it went. These myths, legends, and lore went on

for as long as a missionary would listen. And it seemed the Cheyenne could talk forever.

But the missionaries were made of stern stuff. They gave as well as they got. And the focus of their efforts—an unfortunate choice, as it turned out—fell on the Cheyenne concept of heaven, Seyan, where all the Cheyenne dead were indiscriminately sent, where there was no Judgment. That seemed to be the keystone of Cheyenne beliefs, the cornerstone upon which all else was built. Take that away, and all the rest were sure to follow.

Thus the missionaries began by introducing the concepts of sin and judgment and, most important, hell, that infernal region that existed somewhere below the surface of the earth, where *sinners*—nonbelievers in the white man's God—would live amid eternal flames.

"There is no *good* god, no *good* spirit," the missionaries insisted, "that lives below the surface of the earth. The one God above controls the heavens and the earth's surface, but *below* the surface there is but *evil*, there are only Satan and all the sinners and nonbelievers among you."

McElroy's perorations were the most effective, since he seemed able to give the best imitation of Lucifer, besides being the loudest. Agent Mallory was heard to say that when McElroy was in full voice, every Indian within fifty miles was in danger of being saved.

"Beware, my red brothers," said McElroy, and the Cheyenne were instantly on their guard. "Unless you convert, you shall surely spend eternity stoking the devil's fires."

This was, of course, not the happiest of predictions, nor easily demonstrable, nor immune to inquiry.

"Black Robe," asked one Cheyenne, "we know that you bury your dead in the ground. Is that because they are all sinners?"

McElroy countered that one with a patronizing smile.

"Black Robe," called out another, "how would we get to this place of fire and wicked gods? We know the way to Seyan, it is along the Milky Way. But what path leads to . . . hell?"

"Take the trail west and turn right at the first dead tree," muttered Mallory, and the Reverend Pilcher glared at him.

"Your shadow will know how to get there," answered Reverend McElroy cleverly and triumphantly.

At that point a Cheyenne Contrary said, "This man is wise. Let us stay and hear more." Whereupon the Reverend McElroy was hit with a small piece of dry dung and the whole crowd got up and tramped off.

"I think you were getting to them," said Pilcher.

McElroy glared at Pilcher.

"Anybody seen Amy Selby?" asked Mallory, and McElroy transferred his glare to him.

"Beware, my son," said McElroy. "Sister Selby is a young woman of gleaming virtue."

"So I'm finding out," grumped Mallory. "What's next on the agenda?"

"A rest, then more of the same. I think they're weakening."

"Oh, yeah?" Mallory said. He hadn't seen any such signs. Then the agent's eyes caught movement in the distance, to the west. Wagons were approaching. "Now what's *this*?" he wondered aloud. "More of you people?"

"No, nor had we anticipated any competition."

"Hell," said Mallory, "those are army wagons. I wonder what the hell they want?"

The Sanitary Corps wagons slowly approached and pulled up in front of the agency. Mallory went out to greet them and encountered the corps commander, Colonel Billingsgate. He was not himself a medical man; that function seemed to be reserved for the junior officers of the Sanitary Corps.

"You're the agent?" Billingsgate inquired.

"Yep. Mallory. Who are you?"

"Sanitary Corps, mister, here to clean up and save the heathen, if the missionaries haven't turned them into Sunday Wonders already."

"Nope. Ain't gonna, neither. Scare 'em off the reservation, maybe."

"Well, before they go, we've got business with them."

"Meaning?" Mallory prodded the colonel.

"Vaccinate them against smallpox and teach them how to . . . ummm . . . properly take a dump. You get my meaning?"

"You mean how to *crap*? Always figgered that came natural, a gift from God, as it were."

Billingsgate smiled at him indulgently. "Missionaries gettin' to you, are they?"

"Yes and no. There's one *I* been tryin' to get to. . . ." His voice trailed off. "All right, what's the routine?"

"We'll dig the latrines first, get them used to us being around."

Mallory grinned. "They'll never get used to you being

around. Nothing personal, but up until just recent they was tryin' to *kill* you, and you them. Why, some of these boys, a lot of 'em in fact, were up there at Little Big Horn givin' Custer the treatment. Incidentally, if any of them start waxin' kinda nostalgic for the Greasy Grass..."

"Greasy Grass?"

"That's what they call the Little Big Horn, so..."

"Better not start waxin' nostalgic around *me*. I'll give them something greasy to deal with."

Mallory wondered what the hell this fat oaf Billingsgate could have in mind. The future was looking less rosy by the minute.

"Anyway, first we'll dig the latrines, teach them what they're for and how to use them—"

"What *are* they for?"

Billingsgate stared at him, then sniffed the air. "Haven't you got a *nose*, man? It was all right, when these folks were strollin' across the prairie, to stop and squat, but they're going to be living here for quite some time, and if they don't start using latrines, pretty soon they won't have anyplace to step without steppin' in it. Not to mention the smell...

"Once they're used to us being around, and the latrines are being dug, some maybe using them already, we'll vaccinate them. Four, five days, and we'll be gone."

He walked off to organize things. Mallory called after him, "Keep an eye out for the Contraries."

Colonel Billingsgate looked back quizzically, but Mallory just smiled. He could find out for himself.

And the colonel *did* find out when he tried to get a Contrary to help with the digging. "Go over there and dig," said the colonel, and the man said, "Yes," and headed for the hills, so to speak.

But by afternoon the excavation of the latrines, by complaining white and reluctant Cheyenne musclepower, was well under way. At which point several doctors, including Lieutenant Marlowe, emerged from a large tent—an American medicine lodge—waving long, sharp needles.

The Cheyenne gave those needles long, sharp looks.

While the four doctors and their assistants stood by, Colonel Billingsgate attempted to explain to the Cheyenne chiefs, elders, and medicine men the scientific rationale behind the vaccinations.

You deliberately infect a subject with a weak strain of a

disease, explained Billingsgate, or in this case a strain from a similar but harmless disease, cowpox, and the subject's system then creates the antibodies that render the subject immune to a serious and possibly fatal attack of the target disease.

It wasn't an easy concept to get across. Even among the Sanitary Corps there were some doubting Thomases, and even Colonel Billingsgate, deathly afraid of needles, had avoided inoculation thus far, avoided it like the pox itself. Consequently, in view of the less than total commitment among the Sanitary Corps itself, and Colonel Billingsgate's understandably less than fiery exhortation, it was no wonder that the Cheyenne did not hurry to line up to be jabbed.

Instead, they fell back and huddled in groups and began to exchange dark suspicions. This is how they saw the situation: First the Black Robes descend upon them to try to convert them to the Black Robes' religion. When that fails, other Americans show up with their Long Needles, clearly to punish the Cheyenne for not being converted, possibly even to annihilate them for their resistance. Why else would they be digging the big holes? To dump the dead Cheyenne into, that's why, killed by the Long Needles, dump them in as a way of speeding their passage down into the bowels of the earth to the white man's hell.

They retired to consider appropriate action.

In the meantime, in one part of the village, a latrine pit had been dug and a modest hut placed over it. One of the diggers, Private Crispin, a true believer in the cause of latrines and vaccinations, stood back to admire the edifice. "Mr. Lo sure oughta appreciate *that*," he announced at large. But then he saw no one queuing up in front of the outhouse. "Maybe it ain't the right time of day," he surmised hopefully. But then he saw a Cheyenne emerge from a tipi and start to slip behind it, loosening his buckskin trousers as he went.

Crispin saw a chance to make a convert. He raced to the tipi, circled it, and caught the Cheyenne just as the poor man had assumed a squatting position.

"Ha!" cried Crispin, coming as close to a war cry as that camp had heard in quite some time.

The Cheyenne, though severely shocked by the cry, was also galvanized into movement, shooting erect, drawing his trousers up. Unfortunately, though, the evacuation process was already under way.

The Cheyenne, after his breathing had returned to normal,

stared at Crispin gloomily, feeling uncomfortable.

"Oh. Too late, huh? Gee, that's kinda terrible. . . ."

The Cheyenne continued to stare at him, eyes hardening to agates, lips compressing.

"Next time," said Crispin airily, not realizing how close to injury he'd come, "that's what th' latrine's for. You understand? Latrine? You crap in *there*!"

Crispin then turned on his heel and walked away. He could be heard yelling to his buddies, "Hey, what's the Cheyenne word for 'crap'?"

five ⎯⎯⎯⎯⎯⎯⎯⎯⎯⎯

It was a few days later, lazy days for Easy Company.

"Heard anything about the payroll, Sergeant?" asked Captain Conway. "Late again this month?"

"Not as far as I know, sir," answered Ben Cohen from behind his desk.

"Nice if it came a little early this time," mused Warner Conway, standing in the door to his office, "now that we've got all the men here on post. Get it all over with in one operation instead of having to wait for patrols to come dribbling in."

"Mmmm," agreed Cohen, doodling on a pad.

"Hear anything from the reservation, from Mallory?"

"Aw, hell," said Cohen, "nothin' the army does makes the BIA happy. He thinks the Cheyenne are bein' rushed awful fierce. Missionaries have got 'em seeing their shadows all over the place, and Mallory figures that if the Cheyenne were allowed to step in their own crap a while, they'd dig their own trenches without the help of the Sanitary Corps."

"Well, that's true enough," agreed Conway. "But without

42

the vaccines, there might not be any Cheyenne left to do any dumping, let alone dig latrines."

"Guess you're right, sir.... Yeah? What do you want?"

Amos Fletcher had stuck his ugly, red-eyed head into the orderly room. "Jes' checkin' fer messages, Sarge. Cranmore? Anxious to get movin' south."

Cohen glanced at Bradshaw, who shook his head. "We'll let you know, Cranmore, soon's one comes in." Fletcher nodded. "Who are you joining up with down there?"

"Church group. Some right devoted Christian folk."

"That so?" muttered Cohen. Ben was Jewish, but his wife, Maggie, was freethinking Irish Catholic, so Ben had come to know his faiths and sects. "What denomination?"

"Small group outa the Carolina hills. Call themselves Sybarites. The Sybaritic Temple? You've heard of it?"

"Can't say as I have," said Ben Cohen as he heard Matt Kincaid shoving his chair around.

Matt appeared in his office doorway. Fletcher was gone. "Did I hear right?" asked Matt. "Sybarites?"

Conway, frowning in puzzlement, said, "I'm trying to place it."

"Sybaritic means luxurious, sensual."

Conway grinned. "Church of luxury? Sensual? Sounds like your kind of church, Matt."

"How'd you know that word, sir?" asked Ben Cohen.

"You know, Sergeant Cohen," said Matt heavily, "we officers *did* go to school. And we weren't only taught military tactics."

"Yeah, yeah, if you say so, sir," said Cohen. "But Mr. Fox must've missed a lesson or two here or there. He damn near got his foot shot off out at the range this mornin'."

"He shot his own *foot*?"

"Just the toe off the boot. He was practicin' his"—he paused to underscore the sarcasm—"his quick draw."

"Fox?" exclaimed Matt.

"Yep. 'Course, Mr. Smaldoon was showin' him how, and lent Mr. Fox one of his pistols."

"The short-barreled Smith & Wesson?"

"Yep. The one with the hair trigger."

"Smaldoon's a prince," said Captain Conway.

"Almost got rid of his roommate," said Cohen.

"How's that working out—Fox and Smaldoon together?" asked Captain Conway.

"Smaldoon hits the sack at about eight or nine," said Matt. "Fox keeps the lamp burning till midnight or after, reading. It's working out just fine."

"What does Fox read? Manuals?"

"Hardly, sir. He's got a bunch of Wild West magazines."

"Oh, my God," breathed Captain Conway.

"That's probably why he's practicing his fast draw."

There suddenly came the sound of a muffled gunshot from close by the orderly room. Matt got out the door first, followed by Captain Conway. Ben Cohen made a quick surge that moved his desk a foot or two, but then he just settled back in his chair.

Matt made a quick guess and burst into Second Lieutenant Maynard Fox's quarters, which were now being shared by Second Lieutenant Smaldoon.

Smaldoon stood on one side of the main room, inspecting the furrow made by a bullet on both the inside of his upper left arm and his ribcage, both furrows about a quarter-inch deep. He looked up at Matt, a bemused expression on his face.

On the other side of the room, Mr. Fox—long nose, intelligent eyes, black hair lying flat on his head, tall but slim and wiry—examined the short-barreled Smith & Wesson that lay in his hand. His was an expression of wonderment. He looked up at Matt and Captain Conway and said, "I didn't hardly do more than *look* at it and it went off." He extended the gun toward Matt, so he could take a close look. Matt Kincaid had a damn fast draw himself, faster than anyone he'd yet gone up against, but never had his right hand moved faster than it did as he snatched the gun from Fox's hand.

Naturally the damn thing went off again, making Smaldoon giggle, making Captain Conway step back a quick pace, and bringing a pleased smile to Fox's face. "See?" said Fox.

Matt Kincaid eyed the shattered mirror. Then he turned to Smaldoon and roared, "Goddammit, Smaldoon, you fix this gun up right or I'm going to load it up, strap it to your goddamn crotch, and make you *sleep* with it."

Matt cleared the gun's chambers, closed it with a snap of his wrist, and then snapped his wrist again, slinging the pistol toward Smaldoon.

Smaldoon plucked it neatly from the air.

Got to admit, thought Matt, the man knows how to handle his weapons.

"Just some slight adjustments," murmured Smaldoon.

Captain Conway nodded benignly. "How are you two getting along?"

Fox puckered his brow while Smaldoon cast him a sidelong glance. "Just some slight adjustments," repeated Smaldoon quietly. Then, "Hasn't that bastard died yet?"

"Not if your sister has anything to say about it," Conway replied.

It was true. Cassandra Smaldoon was just about knocking herself out, tending to the wounded man.

A small bedroom and a slightly larger living room comprised the Smaldoon quarters. Normally, Cassie Smaldoon slept in the bedroom while her brother bedded down outside. Now the stranger was in her brother's bed and Cassie had dragged hers from the bedroom so she could keep constant watch.

"I trust you still change your clothes in your bedroom?" her brother had commented.

"Oh, yes. Not that it would make any difference. He's still unconscious."

But he was showing signs of awakening. His eyes were beginning to move beneath the closed lids. And he'd toss mildly and random, unintelligible sounds would emanate from his mouth.

His lips were cracked, and stayed cracked no matter how many times Cassie dampened them.

He soon started speaking more clearly. Single words—"sickness," "pus," "evil," "Rachel"—several times. And then, "Why, God, oh why?" also repeated to the point of becoming a chant.

The most disturbing to Cassie was "Rachel," or combinations involving "Rachel." Sounded like he was pretty close to some woman. And then there were some other names she thought she heard, might have been the names of children. *His* children, probably. Damn! She was probably nursing a happily married father of twelve.

But that didn't sound like a bounty hunter, and that was what Matt and Ben Cohen said he seemed to be.

For that matter, a bounty hunter didn't sound very nice, like a human buzzard feeding off society's carrion. That was what Matt had said. Of course, then he'd said the "carrion" was alive and able to defend itself, so maybe that was a little different.

But either way, a bounty hunter didn't much resemble a

gold-braided cavalry officer, one of her frequent fantasy lovers. But hell, at least this one was brave, a real man, and might even look good beneath that stubble.

She'd have liked to shave him, but she'd never shaved a man and wasn't about to practice on one that had already lost a lot of blood. Maybe—

"Who are you?"

Her eyes popped wide open and she whirled about. The man in the bed had raised his head. "Rachel? Is that you?"

And then his head fell back, his eyes closed, and he said no more.

Ten minutes later Maggie Cohen entered, carrying a bucket of steaming water and some clean bandages. Cassie told her of the momentary consciousness of their guest.

Maggie shook her head. "Talk about *tough*. The men really admire him, even your brother, though he'd never say so. There's not a man worth his salt that'll let death get the best of him without one hell of a fight."

Cassie nodded, then said, "Could you shave him?"

"Sure. But let's get him washed and the bandages changed first." She turned back the cover and started to strip the pajamas, Lieutenant Fox's pajamas, from the man. "Maybe you'd better wait in the bedroom again. Your brother—"

"I don't give a damn about my brother. I'm not hiding anymore. I've seen a naked man before."

"I should hope so," muttered Maggie.

They stripped and bathed him, changed the bandages, and then clothed him again. "Appears to be healing nicely. Nothing green or rotten showing," Maggie said cheerfully.

She was gone for a while, and then was back with Ben's razor. "Ben got both his arms broke once. I had to shave him for close to two months. He swore he'd never break so much as a finger after that." She grinned. "Our friend here, being unconscious, should make it real easy. . . . Oh, *hell*. Dab that with some cotton, will you, Cass?"

In the meantime, Stretch Dobbs was doing what he did best— lying down. Six foot seven inches of lying down. On this occasion he'd found himself a commodious patch of ground between the stables and the sutler's, sort of hidden from the orderly room, where he could catch the afternoon rays of sunshine. *Jes' a quick li'l ol' nap*, he thought.

His eyes had been closed just briefly when a shadow passed over the sun . . . except he didn't recall seeing any clouds. . . . The first sergeant! His eyes snapped open.

"Hi."

The sun was behind her, casting her in shadow, outlining her shape. Stretch felt a sudden urge to leap up. "H'lo," he said. "Who're you?"

"Billie," she said. "That's short for William. My folks wanted a boy, a man. . . . Me too."

"Me too?"

"Want a man. I want a man too."

Stretch tried to assemble his thoughts. This young lady was a mite more forward and a hell of a lot more sudden than he was accustomed to. "Well . . ."

"Those stables sure look cool," she said.

"Yeah," said Stretch, thinking that they were also full of manure that he and Malone were supposed to be collecting.

"And dark," she added.

"Hell," said Stretch, "Nothin' t' be scared of."

"Scared? *I* ain't scared. *You* scared?"

"Me? Scared?" He laughed.

"Let's go," she said.

"Go? Go where?" He looked around for his buddy. Malone ought to be in on this, he thought.

Malone *was* in on it, in a way.

He was stationed over by the mess, where he'd gone for water, and maybe some coffee, for himself and Dobbs. While inside he'd seen Corporal Medford, a squad leader in Chubb's Third Platoon, sucking up to the cooks as usual, trying to get favors. Thought he was slick about it and no one knew, but everyone knew. Medford made himself out to be the most righteous, God-fearing, moral man on post, but everyone knew, when he happened to be on guard and was checking out the guard post, how he'd stop by the stovepipes over the married quarters and turn his ears inside out trying to hear something.

Now Medford had acquired himself a tail. He didn't know it yet, but Malone was waiting for him to find out.

The "tail" was one of the gals from the scroungy group that had ridden in a few days before. Malone had seen some disease in his time, as a boy, and his folks had told him a lot of scary stories from the old country. He knew what to avoid. Besides, this bunch stank nearly as much as some of his army buddies, especially Arnold, which of course made it hard for *them* to realize anything was wrong.

But anyway, one of the gals had set her cap for Corporal Medford and was sort of following him around.

Gals *never* followed Medford around, so he didn't notice. Not yet anyway. But it was just a matter of time.

Malone wished something would happen soon. Stretch was probably dying of thirst, and the coffee was getting cold. Maybe he could run to the stables and get back—

Uh-oh. Medford was heading for the latrine, walking super-slow the way he always did when he was headin' off to take a crap. Malone wondered why, at those times, he always walked so slow. Must be embarrassed or something.

But anyway, the scroungy gal was slinking right after him. Medford looked over his shoulder, right at her, but didn't even notice that she was there. Not consciously, anyway, though his stride seemed to perk up a mite. Maybe he was heading in there to beat his joint to death, thought Malone.

Medford entered the latrine and closed the door carefully. The scroungy gal stepped up to the door, looked around with a grin, then opened the door enough to slide inside, closing it behind her.

Malone's eyes barely had time to widen, his lungs hardly time to fill before the latrine door practically blew off its hinges.

Corporal Medford came out like he'd been catapulted, his trousers around his knees, his suspenders flapping, and his prick bouncing around every which way. Inside the latrine, Malone could see, the scroungy gal was standing with her skirt hiked up around her waist . . . wearing nothing underneath it.

And then, with a smile, she closed the door.

Malone went bouncing off toward the stables, laughing like crazy, sloshing water from the bucket and trying to retain some of the coffee in the two cups he held.

He reached the stables, but Stretch was nowhere in sight.

Then he heard, "Wal, I dunno, someone might show up of a sudden. Maybe later on, when it gets dark. . . . Well, hell, I know it's *dark*, but maybe it oughta be *darker* . . . an' there's a funny smell. . . ."

Jesus, one of them's got poor Stretch, Malone thought as he raced into the stables and burst upon Stretch just as he was about to settle onto and into Billie.

"Stretch!"

Dobbs scrambled upright, planting a foot square in Billie's gut, thinking the voice had the ring of the Lord God Almighty, probably acting on a tip from that shit, Medford. He rattled around the stall, sending a bay gelding stampeding toward Malone.

Malone dodged the horse, then stepped in close.

The girl, shameless, just lay there with her legs spread. Malone had only to glance. He'd seen stuff like it before, the rash, that swelling. He was going to have to tell Stretch exactly what that "funny smell" was. "You stuck her yet, dumbbell?"

"Hell, Malone, how could I, with you jumpin' in, shoutin' to near scare me half to death."

"Good. Pull up your pants and get outside. Wash yourself up real good. There's some water, and maybe some coffee, if I didn't spill it."

"An' what're *you* gonna do? You gonna git some?"

"Get outa here, Stretch!" roared Malone, and Stretch, who was big, all right, but good-natured and obedient, especially when it came to his bad-tempered Irish buddy, did as he'd been told. Then Malone turned back to the girl, Billie, who hadn't moved an inch.

He stared down at her, waiting for some sign of modesty or embarrassment, but in vain. Then he said, "All right, me girl, you can wave that thing o' yours around all you want— likely makes you happy makin' others feel as poorly as you do—but you be wavin' it at any o' *my* buddies an' there'll be hell to pay, if you get my meanin'."

She sat up and pulled her skirt down to cover her nakedness, staring at him with dead eyes. "I ain't tryin' to hurt nobody," she said dully. "I was prettier 'fore I got sick," she added, brushing her matted hair back from her eyes, "but there ain't nothin' really wrong with me, not really, is there?"

Malone, tough as he was, couldn't take this. He turned and walked from the stables.

"Is there?" the girl cried shrilly, and that cry followed him for several days.

six ─────────────────────

At the first light of dawn, Two Moons cautiously peeked from his tipi. His three wives still lay slumbering, as did his children (the next time he raised a tipi he was going to make it a larger one, even though he might have to use some of the agent's canvas tarpaulins). Two Moons eyed his children, five of varying ages. Two others had died very young. Perhaps some of these would also—the gods were capricious—in which case he wouldn't need the larger tipi.

He peeked out again. The Black Robes were up and about, as were the Long Needles. Didn't they ever sleep?

Damned little, as a matter of fact. The Black Robes, McElroy in particular, had spent the night wondering where the Sanitary Corps was hiding the Cheyenne. McElroy had called for a big service along the lines of a revival meeting—he'd imported three rascally Indians who knew the language and could pass for Cheyenne, who were going to be "converted," thus encouraging the rest, but no one had showed up.

Meanwhile, the Long Needles were wondering where the

hell the missionaries had hidden the Cheyenne.

But the frustration and mystery was all because the Cheyenne were creeping about with the utmost of stealth. They'd held a council meeting and decided that neither the Black Robes nor the Long Needles should be encouraged, that they should be shunned and avoided, and perhaps they would go away. This decision surprised Crying Eagle and his friends among the youthful firebrands. It was a good decision and they would join in shunning the Americans.

But they didn't stop there. Crying Eagle and his friends had become, like many of the younger Indians from all tribes, cynical when it came to dealing with the Americans. They did not truly believe that the Americans would give up so readily. The fat, loud American who led the Long Needles had clearly eaten enough to last him through the Seasons of Yellow and Brown Grass and even through the Season of the Snowblind; his size seemed to add weight to his purpose and determination in the Cheyenne's eyes.

Therefore, Crying Eagle and his friends took care to keep their rifles cleaned and oiled and, along with their ammunition, hidden but ready at hand. The guns were a show of confidence by the BIA, intended for the securing of buffalo and game; the Indian bureau was not so foolish as to think that it could change, overnight, the focus of Cheyenne culture from hunting to horticulture, though they'd do their damnedest.

"Which means, mostly," explained Agent Mallory to Amy Selby, whom he'd caught by means of stationing himself outside her tent before dawn, "that they get a whole lot of food that don't taste good to them. Some of these folk ain't never eaten nothing but meat. These Plains tribes, once they hit the Plains—oh, a century or so ago—and started moving all the time, never stayed nowhere long enough to grow anything. These people are meat-eaters. But the BIA's determined they're gonna *try* to change 'em, make 'em grow their own food, stuff like that. But you oughta see Cheyenne starin' at a plate of beans . . . an' you oughta *hear* 'em afterwards. . . ."

Mallory thought that was pretty funny, but Amy Selby didn't crack a smile. Mallory decided that she was a mite more delicate of temperament than he'd guessed.

"Of course, that's what my men say. I don't go in for that crude kind of humor myself."

Now Amy wondered what kind of humor he was talking about. Agent Mallory was a very strange man, and a very

51

persistent one. She'd had occasion to use one of the new latrines herself that morning, when the call of nature had raised her from her cot well before anyone else was up and about. Except, most cursed of surprises, this man Mallory, who had been standing outside her tent and who had *followed* her to the latrine. She'd practically had to close the latrine door in his face.

Then, while tending with dignity and care to her natural functions—and delicacy was time-consuming—he'd had the nerve to stand outside and shout, "Y'all *died* in there?"

Coincidentally, just as she recalled that upsetting moment, and while Agent Mallory was droning on about something or other, there came a hideous shriek.

Mallory shot to his feet, his blood running cold, his heart nearly coming to a dead stop. He took two steps toward the agency door, but then stopped, took several deep breaths, turned around, and returned to the table, smiled at Miss Selby, lifted and drained his coffee cup . . . and then turned and ran like hell out the door.

Once outside, he breathed easier. It was just the Long Needles, up to their fun and games, striking terror into the hearts of the Cheyenne.

They'd caught about ten Cheyenne, Two Moons and family, caught them huddling in their tipi, hiding beneath robes. They were now dragging the family members out—the youngest and weakest first—taking firm hold and jabbing their long needles into them. The Cheyenne, even the youngest, answered their cooing reassurances with savage looks of pure hate.

The doctors finished with the family and decided to take a break. Marlowe wandered over to chat with the agent. "I'm going to have to start recruiting my assistants from the army wrestling teams," said Marlowe. "Do you have any idea why they're so frightened?"

"Sure do. Don't you?" Mallory replied.

"Not at all. It's pretty simple. We explained it to them in words a child could understand."

"But that child you're thinking of doesn't have several centuries of religious beliefs tellin' him different, *nor* does that child have these missionaries scarin' him to death."

"Scaring them how? By promising them heaven?"

"They already got that, doc. The missionaries are scarin' them by promisin' them *hell* if they don't convert. And the missionaries are telling them that hell is somewhere under the ground. Then you people come along with your long, skinny knives—"

"Knives?"

"Your *needles*. To kill 'em with, either jab 'em to death or poison them—mind you, this is the way that *they're* seeing things—and then you got your men and them digging holes in the ground to help them on their way to hell. Now the Indian don't bury his dead, but he knows the white man does. So what the hell is he to think, all these big *graves* being dug?"

Marlowe understood, and didn't blame the Cheyenne. "These goddamned missionaries," he growled. "Can't you get rid of them, Mallory?"

"How? You want me to tell them that we, that I, that me and the Cheyenne, don't want no Christianity? You want me to start lookin' for another job? Besides"—he smiled winningly—"there's this one little female missionary and . . . Oh, Christ, I'll bet she got away on me."

He turned and ran for the agency, bursting in on Amy Selby in such a manner as to cause her to spill coffee on her robe. "Oh, hell, you better get that off," suggested Agent Mallory unwisely.

Lieutenant Marlowe turned back to survey the scene of the recent inoculation. The family huddled about outside their tipi, as if death were imminent. Marlowe felt badly about the whole affair, even though he knew that Two Moons and his large, polygamous family would not die from smallpox. But if Marlowe's survey had taken in a bit of the future, as well as the past and present, he would have felt a whole lot worse.

The obvious devastation of Two Moons and his family had been the last straw. Those well-oiled Spencer repeaters were being taken from hiding and loaded. Even old Two-Leg Bear, onetime war chief, unearthed an ancient musket with which, since it was hammerless, he planned to club someone. If he could just totter close enough to touch, to count coup one last time, he would die happy . . . and Heammawihio would be pleased. One god indeed. The Black Robes must think them simple.

Wrongheaded, yes, but not simple. Colonel Billingsgate had emerged that morning to find the corpse of an owl impaled on a stake driven into the ground before his tent. He had inquired of the Reverend Pilcher, since no one in the Sanitary Corps could explain it.

"Owls are, among other things, symbols of death," the Reverend Pilcher had said, beaming. "Picking one's way through the tortuous tangle of myth and symbol and rite that is the Cheyenne belief, that is no child's play. Theirs is a complex religion. Which is the problem. A simpler belief would be far easier to defeat. These people have answers, and gods, for *everything*."

In reply to which Billingsgate, with a rare flash of insight, had muttered sarcastically, "Poor Mr. Lo. Poor, simple, misguided Mr. Lo."

"Huh," grunted Pilcher. "The Cheyenne have more guidance than they know what to do with."

Unfortunately for everyone, some of that "guidance" was on the prowl.

Private Crispin was making his early rounds, searching out candidates for the latrines. They didn't dig those goddamn latrines for nothing! But so far he'd had no luck. For all he knew, Mr. Lo was starving himself so he wouldn't have to use these new facilities—that'd be just like those dumb bastards.

Private Crispin had been an only child of fastidious, if simple, parents. And as an adult he was just as fastidious, if just as simple. In fact he was a hygienic zealot. He didn't know he was that, of course, in those words, and he realized that there weren't many like him. But there'd be more if he had anything to say about it.

A movement caught Crispin's eye. A Cheyenne, clearly searching for an unused patch of ground. Crispin dashed toward him, cursing the turds upon which he was, of necessity, having to step. "Help!" he cried as he fell upon the startled Cheyenne. "Gimme a hand!" he implored, figuring he might have his hands full dragging the struggling Cheyenne to the nearest latrine.

Just one man answered his summons, Private Belcher, but between the two of them they got the Cheyenne moving smartly in the right direction.

As the wooden hut loomed large, the Cheyenne, who was the young warrior Yellow Bead, saw where they were taking him—the entrance to the Black Robes' hell—and he figured the Long Needles were waiting for him close by, and he started screaming his head off.

"Feller do make quite a racket," commented Private Belcher, grinning.

The grin dissolved instantly as a .45-caliber slug from a Spencer repeater entered his back and split his breastbone coming out.

Blood and flesh splattered over Yellow Bead and Private Crispin as the boom of the shot reached them.

Crying Eagle stood some fifty yards away, the Spencer still at his shoulder. Crispin stared at him, loosening his grip on Yellow Bead. Then he let go completely, forgot about the Scoffs he was packing, and turned and took off as fast as he could.

Crying Eagle took out after him, carrying the Spencer in one hand and, more importantly, his war axe in the other. Shooting the American had brought no honor, but with this one he would count coup.

But maybe not the first coup. Yellow Bead had grasped the situation quickly, and he too had taken off after Private Crispin, dragging his long knife out as he ran, and he had a head start on Crying Eagle.

Private Crispin had always displeased his father with his slowness afoot, or displeased him until his father had accepted reality and changed his tack, saying, "You may not be the fastest, Robert, but you will always be the one to finish." Now it looked like he was about to lose on both scores. Where the hell were the rest of the men?

Most of them were back at the main camp where, having finished most of the latrines, they were waiting for the Cheyenne to wise up and come to be vaccinated. They heard the shot and thought, or hoped, that it was just someone shooting some game.

But then they heard the growing number of yips and shouts, growing more numerous and louder, and then they saw flashes of army blue as Crispin tried to dodge and dash in and out among the tipis.

They started grabbing for their weapons as they recognized Crispin and shouted encouragement—"Get the goddamn lead out, Rob!"

Unfortunately, Rob didn't, or couldn't. He'd almost rounded the last tipi between himself and the men of the Sanitary Corps when Yellow Bead caught up with him and slid his long knife surely in between Crispin's ribs. He fell to the side, caving in part of Two Moons' tipi.

Yellow Bead cried, "I'm first!" and bent over to finish the job by scalping Crispin.

Crying Eagle, arriving and whacking away at Crispin's skull with his war axe and crying, "I'm second!" almost crushed Yellow Bead's hand with the same blow.

A Sanitary Corps soldier, crouched some distance away, said, "Jesus, the feller's dead already. Why're they still choppin' at him?"

Yellow Bead tore off the scalp, a huge hunk, traditionally much larger than usual, damn near the size of a wig.

But then Yellow Bead was hit by a curtain of bullets fired by enraged Sanitary Corps soldiers. He slammed to the ground, but was dead before he hit.

Those few bullets that missed him tore holes in Two Moons' tipi. Two Moons peeked out with extreme caution, then quickly reached out with his war axe and hit the still body of Private Crispin. "I'm third!" cried Two Moons, but he wasn't certain anybody heard him.

That was because the battle was being waged hot and heavy. The corpsmen had flattened out, those that had guns and knew how to fight, and were giving about as good as they got. But the rest of the Cheyenne began to arrive and everyone took off, as best they could, for the agency buildings, where the agent and his several civilian helpers had already begun setting themselves up in comfortable firing positions.

Luckily for the soldiers, and the missionaries who had taken cover among them, once they started running for the agency, clearly exposing themselves, the firing from the Cheyenne side let up.

The Cheyenne didn't honor coups struck from a distance. Thus, when the enemy got up and made their run for safety, the Cheyenne lit out after them, though not exactly *after* them, rather at an angle trying to cut off the line of retreat. And they damn near did cut them off, which would have led to quite a slaughter. They didn't because Mallory and his men cut loose a sustained and withering fire.

The Cheyenne charge stumbled and stopped, and then fell back out of accurate rifle range. They didn't have to be very bright to realize the Americans weren't going anywhere. They could surround them and wait.

"They're already cuttin' the telegraph wire," said Mallory. "Someone get out the back," he cried, "before they get us completely surrounded. Ride like hell for Easy."

"I'll go," grumbled Forrest, a man who hadn't joined the Sanitary Corps in order to do a lot of Indian fighting. What was going on right then was more than he'd bargained for.

Mallory considered the situation; it looked like *he* was going to have to give the go-ahead. Colonel Billingsgate, or what was left of him, was lying about sixty yards distant, having had about eighty coups counted on him; in the race for safety his appetite, and a mess of Cheyenne, had finally caught up to him; this was one fatty who wouldn't die of heart congestion.

Mallory saw that Forrest was a big man, though, unlike Billingsgate, he'd fairly flown over the ground, and would probably slow even a good army horse down. A smaller man would be better. But there was no time. And there were no other volunteers. "All right, get going."

"I'm going too," blurted Amy Selby, having understood Mallory's hesitation.

"You jes' keep down outa sight," Mallory said.

"I can ride," said Amy. "Real well . . . and I'm *light*."

Mallory thought quickly. If no one got through, Amy Selby's scalp was up for grabs anyway.

"Better let her go," muttered Marlowe, at the agent's elbow.

Mallory decided, and nodded toward Amy, who then slipped out the back after Forrest.

"How does this thing work?" asked Marlowe, holding on to one of the many conversions of the old Springfield musket. "Looks like you've got to load it each time."

"You do," growled Mallory. "The Cheyenne have got all the new repeaters."

A bullet whistled in through the window overhead.

"It's hell in a real fight," the agent went on, "loadin' an' firin', loadin' an' firin'. Usually, even in a company of soldiers, there're just a few men that are real good. Most times, a man gets off a shot or two and runs, or he's busy tryin' to load up when a hostile walks up and buries an axe in his head.

"The hostiles, though, even back before cartridges, were real good, ridin' along with their mouths full of lead balls, throwin' powder into the gun on the run and spittin' balls down the barrel an' rammin' 'em home. Jes' couldn't shoot real good, 'specially from their ponies, but they'd sure get off a lot of shots."

Marlowe studied him as Mallory rattled on. Nerves, Marlowe concluded.

This conclusion was borne out when Mallory concluded shakily, "Sure hope that gal gets through safe."

It was close. Amy Selby, coming out of the back of the agency, saw Forrest running for a nearby corral, dragging a saddle—no one had been out riding, and none of the horses were saddled. She ran after him.

The corral was small and the horses, though a trifle spooked, had heard gunfire before and were reasonably calm. Forrest caught a horse fast, whipped a bridle onto it, and then threw the saddle up over its back, without benefit of a blanket.

Amy caught hers quickly too, and got the bridle on rapidly, her hands remembering her childhood farm days better than her mind did. She began to lead the horse, a big, powerful chestnut, back to the agency, where the saddles were piled. Forrest was finishing up his saddling. She happened to glance west and saw a few dusky forms nipping through the high grass. *Oh, gracious*, she thought, and clawed her way up onto the horse.

From her higher vantage point she could see the circle around the agency rapidly being closed. "C'mon, mister!" she shouted at Forrest, and kicked her horse into a gallop.

Forrest guessed what was happening and mounted with remarkable speed for a big man, lighting out after Amy.

The circle was within forty yards of being closed when Amy raced by, riding like an Indian, lying down alongside her horse's neck. But it was just twenty yards wide when Forrest went through, and the Cheyenne, realizing a gunshot was better than no coup at all, cut loose.

Six bullets hit Forrest and he didn't even realize it. They didn't hit anything immediately vital and he was so excited, his adrenaline pumping so hard, that he hardly felt them. A few bumps on the leg, side, and back, that could have been rocks thrown, for all they bothered him.

A quarter-mile farther along, though, he began to feel them, and realized he was leaking like a sieve.

Amy slowed long enough for him to catch up, and she saw his clothes slowly turning red, but didn't say anything. What was there to say?

She looked back and saw that the Cheyenne had mounted and were in pursuit.

Forrest was clinging grimly to his horse, but his sheer weight was slowing the beast. The Cheyenne would catch them soon. *Jesus*, Amy swore to herself, *what is a Christian girl to do?*

Amy glanced over her shoulder. The Cheyenne were getting closer. She was sharp-eyed and could just about distinguish individuals, and she was astonished to see that one rider, daubing himself, was turning blue before her very eyes. She decided the distance was deceiving her.

"Did they make it?" asked Lieutenant Marlowe.

Mallory frowned at him. "Don't know. They didn't go down. But either Forrest is ridin' with a ton of lead in 'im, or them Cheyenne are so cross-eyed we could walk out there and hit 'em over the head. They cut loose at Forrest not ten yards away, it seemed, but he kept on."

"And he was not the religious one," said Marlowe.

"No, but he was the scaredest. Take a cannon to slow *him* down. You can be certain he'll ride till he drops."

"How can you be so sure?"

"After a while you can read their eyes. And I don't know that Forrest feller from a hole in the ground, but out there runnin', he started last and got here first. He was *flyin'*."

"So they might make it."

Mallory's face fell. "If they wasn't being chased by Cheyenne, they might. The Cheyenne can ride with the best of 'em, and they don't give up."

"Sorry I asked."

Mallory looked around. "Wonder if everyone made it?"

"We had a pit crew and a medical team over yonder," said Marlowe. "But I don't see them."

But the Cheyenne had. The pit crew had finished digging the last latrine pit and the medical team was looking for some Cheyenne to vaccinate—not with a great deal of optimism— when they heard the distant gunfire. It defied explanation. The pit detail wanted to hurry back, but the medical team thought that perhaps they should wait, that if anything had happened, they might be safer where they were. In reality, nothing they could have done would have saved them.

While Amy and Forrest were trying to outrun the Cheyenne, a large group of stone-faced, slit-eyed warriors found them.

In less than a minute, eight men were dead—one officer, two noncom assistants, and five privates. Two privates escaped, diving headfirst into the latrine pit and burying themselves.

The eight dead were scalped and thrown into the latrine pit, landing on top of and helping to obscure and save the two privates. Then the needles were discovered in the doctor's bag and were then thrust into the bodies. The corpses fairly bristled with syringes.

Then dirt was thrown in on top of them, but not enough to fill the pit, because the Cheyenne were too anxious to go off and count more coups.

In the meantime, the chase toward Outpost Nine was getting rougher. The Cheyenne had ridden closer, but they'd all hit a stretch of prairie that was not only rolling but strewn with draws and gullies. The Cheyenne would get their quarry lined up in their sights, and suddenly either Amy and Forrest would disappear down into a draw or the Cheyenne would. One brave, Wounded Wing, squeezing off a shot, damn near went over the head of his pony and only managed to blast sand from the bottom of a draw.

Another time a warrior named Big Nose thought he saw a chance to close faster and tried to jump his pony *over* a draw. The pony came up a few feet short and broke both his forelegs. Big Nose left the pony squealing and writhing in pain, and ran after his comrades.

But while he was losing ground, the rest of the Cheyenne braves were gaining. It wouldn't be long now.

But then, coming up out of a draw and seeing a rider not fifty yards away, they were suddenly confronted by the rearing shape of Private Forrest, now dismounted. Forrest wasn't in the steadiest of condition and he didn't know guns, but he had enough strength, or guts, to handle two Scoffs, knew enough to pull triggers, and was determined to take as many of the damned red bastards into the afterlife alongside him as he could.

His Scoffs kept thundering until they were clicking on empties. He dropped them and pulled two more. The Cheyenne kept trying to get close enough to count true coups, but there were only ten of them and Forrest got every last one. In the end he was only able to keep standing because three Cheyenne braves were propped up against him, still feebly struggling.

Forrest looked back to the east through a red haze. He saw a shape running toward him. It was Big Nose, with a battle axe raised high.

Forrest smiled and waited. And it wasn't until Big Nose had run full upon him, as the battle axe was actually denting his skull and as Big Nose's belly was pressing into the snouts of the backup Scoffs, that he pulled the triggers.

Big Nose rose up slightly, jackknifing as the small of his back erupted, and then the two men fell together.

Amy Selby looked back over her shoulder, having heard the roar of gunfire, and saw the pile of corpses around Forrest.

And she saw the finish.

And she raced on again. The tears began to dry as the wind buffeted her face.

seven _____

Amy Selby rode hard, pushing the big chestnut. The horse was enjoying it. It had been a long time since he'd had a good run carrying a real lightweight.

Amy's black robes blew out behind her, billowing to create a deceptive impression of size. Or menace. If she'd been carrying a scythe, a distant viewer might have thought one of the Four Horsemen had gotten loose.

Indeed, despite the absence of the scythe, such a thought did cross the mind of Hiram McClellan as he led his troubled wagon train west. The distant black-robed rider seemed an evil omen.

The Culloch kids, riding the rear wagon, also saw the rider. The youngsters, aged eight, twelve, and nineteen (she was not really a youngster, the oldest, but was treated as one), were shunned by the tribe due to their father's having been crushed by a falling tree and their mother's having died in her last childbirth, both acts clearly the work of the devil. Or perhaps it was simply that the tribe needed its pariahs, preferably three smallish, harmless ones. Shunned and despised, but held captive, as if Hiram were determined to await the appearance of horns and cloven hooves. And as captives, they rode the rear wagon in the company of several dour elders.

They, too, wondered as the rider passed in the distance. Their eyes were sharp and they knew it was a person, a long-haired person, not an omen. It was one of the few people, other than their so-called brethren, that they'd ever seen. But they knew there were more out there, a world full of people, strange and different, but probably a hell of a lot more likeable than those they were forced to live with.

"You children," said one of the elders, a woman with tightly bunned hair, "quit your talking. Hiram spared your lives in exchange for silence. You, Eleanora, should know better, for you are the eldest. Though I suppose," added the elder, "we need not fear any chatter from Enos."

Eleanora stared back at her, her own lips tight with anger. It was only through secret sessions with her eight-year-old brother, Enos, that the boy had even learned to speak.

So secret had it been that no one even guessed that Enos was capable of speech, a deception he happily, or mischievously, maintained.

The elder looked off into the distance, speaking importantly in her harsh, unmusical voice, presumably pronouncing for the ages, "Silence is golden, as you have been taught. Perhaps someday, when Satan releases you from his grip..."

Eleanora didn't believe a word of it, had given up believing years before, soon after she and her brothers had been "sent to Coventry," as their ostracism had been described. Indeed, she wished she had been sent to Coventry. It might have turned out to be a nicer place.

Eleanora Culloch turned back to her brothers, Enos and twelve-year-old Matthew. The brothers had watched the rider disappear into the distance. Both Eleanora and Matthew knew that the rider would not be riding so hard unless he expected to arrive somewhere soon. Which meant that there was some kind of settlement in that direction. Perhaps the time had come....

Eleanora had worriedly watched the measles move slowly through the train. Many were sick and disabled. Thus far the Cullochs' isolation had protected them, but the five men and women who occupied the last wagon with them were beginning to show signs of sickness.

And Eleanora had heard that a small child in the second wagon had died the night before.

Of course it was not true that Amy Selby was riding so hard because she knew there was a settlement close by. She didn't know where Outpost Number Nine was, much less how far distant. She just knew she couldn't slow down, not while the big chestnut—Agent Mallory's favorite and prized horse—was willing to run.

And run he did. Amy Selby had to fight to keep from enjoying the ride. But she rode with the same devotion she brought to any activity. As a child, she'd stayed up seventy-two hours straight to nurse a filly to health, later riding that filly over pastures that rolled like this prairie. Joining the nursing corps, she'd worked herself nearly to death through dedication. And then, having apparently been saved from death herself, not through nursing and medication but through the ministrations of a Presbyterian minister, she'd given her all to God and the Presbyterian cause. Not so much because of God and the Presbyterians, though she certainly was a believer, but rather because she always gave her all.

Now she gave it to the ride. But giving her all to horseback riding involved enjoyment, and that was the problem. She felt a traitor, enjoying the ride, while visions of Forrest going down, or the lifeless face of Reverend Pilcher, lingered in her mind.

But though she was troubled, she was not riding blindly. She was riding west, the way they'd come as best she could recall, and had found a traveled path and followed that, losing sight of the tracks occasionally, but not the frequent heaps of dung.

Finally, in the distance, a tower loomed. And then walls, the ramparts of Outpost Number Nine. She lay down along the horse's neck and the chestnut seemed to sense that there might be some grain, some good oats, awaiting him beyond those distant walls.

Private Tompkins, atop the tower, had spotted the girl as just a speck in the distance, sooner in fact than she'd seen the tower. Moments later Sergeant Breckenridge was beside him, training his Tennessean eyes into the distance. He guessed it might be a missionary only moments before Tompkins not only confirmed it but said it was a girl.

Breckenridge let out a roar that galvanized the entire post and brought Matt Kincaid, Sergeant Cohen, and Captain Conway thundering from the orderly room.

"Missionary gal ridin' like hell," yelled Breckenridge from the tower. "Gotta be trouble over t' the Reservation."

Conway shouted, "Lieutenant Kincaid!" and the entire First Platoon leaped into action. Kincaid generally rode with First Platoon, and they knew that the captain's cry included them. They dashed across the parade, half of them heading for the stable and paddock, the rest moving toward Ordnance.

Matt Kincaid remained standing outside the orderly room. His horse would be brought to him, his and Mister Fox's, already saddled and with rifles hooked to the saddle by their "spider" attachment. Matt liked his hooked to the rear of the saddle; Fox would probably get his hooked up front and likely knock his knee black and blue.

Matt took out first his Scoff and then his second gun, a pearl-handled Colt Peacemaker, and spun the chambers.

Mr. Fox regarded him expectantly, not sure if he was considered part of this action or not. Matt saw his look and merely smiled, adding a barely perceptible nod. Fox immediately started spinning the chambers of *his* guns.

Matt was slowly achieving that deadly calmness with which he preferred to go into battle. Only his eyes slowly moved as the main gate opened and Amy Selby came riding through.

She rode directly for the orderly room, and Matt's eyes slowly filled with admiration as she came closer. He noted how pretty she was, especially with everything wild and flying like that.

She skidded her mount expertly to a halt and Matt saw with pleasant astonishment that she'd ridden bareback.

"'Bout half are dead," she said with no preamble. "The agency's surrounded. They tried to stop us getting here. They killed one of us. He was bad wounded, so he stopped and waited for them. I think he got them all."

"Mallory?" asked Captain Conway.

"He's alive . . . him and the agency people . . . but the Reverend Pilcher—"

"The pink-faced one?"

She nodded.

"And the army colonel."

"Oh, hell," said Conway. "Billingsgate. And he thought he had it knocked."

"He couldn't run very fast," said Amy Selby.

"Run!" squawked Conway. "He could barely *move*."

"Wonder what happened to the telegraph?" said Lieutenant Smaldoon, having raced back from supervising a tactical exercise with Second Platoon's third squad. "And who're you sending, sir?"

"Lieutenant Kincaid's going," Conway said, and Smaldoon's face fell.

"Can't get through," said Sergeant Cohen, coming back out of the orderly room. "Bradshaw tried."

"Line's probably cut," said Matt. "Mr. Lo may not understand the Singing Wire, but he sure knows enough to cut it."

"Oh. They *did*," said Amy suddenly. "The agent said so."

Matt stepped to the side of the chestnut, reached up, and took Amy Selby off the horse before she fell off.

"Take care of that horse, Corporal," said Sergeant Cohen to the man who'd just brought Matt's horse. "And Maggie—"

"We're here," said Flora Conway, the captain's wife, and she and Maggie moved to secure Amy Selby.

"Take your big, manly hands off that poor girl," said Flora smilingly, as she and Maggie got to the pair.

"With reluctance," muttered Matt, and was gratified to see something spark in Amy's eyes, but then he turned away, his face growing hard again. He saw First Platoon mounted and ready, Sergeant Gus Olsen forming them into a column, and Mr. Fox mounting up. Matt leaped astride his horse and had it moving before he was even settled in the saddle.

He led the column out through the gate and looked to the east, and his confidence was rewarded by the sight of Windy Mandalian waiting for them.

Amos Fletcher and his bunch of syphilitics could barely control their glee when they saw Matt ride out with the platoon.

"Hell's bells, Reb," said Amos to one of his cohorts, "we're gonna have to cut them Cheyenne in for part of the take, 'specially if they empty this here post out any more. That payroll's gotta get here soon. Is the month near gone?"

"Aw, shit, Fletch," said Reb. "All ah know is thet it ain't winter an' ah figger spring's past, so . . ."

"You don't even know what *month* it is?"

"Don't you?"

Smaldoon slammed into his quarters and came up short. Cassie was bending tenderly over her patient, dampening his lips with a wet cloth. She looked around in surprise.

"Damn," said Smaldoon. "I forgot I didn't live here any-more."

"Clay? What's wrong?"

Clay Smaldoon replied sulkily, "They've got some action out there, and instead of me they sent Matt Kincaid, which isn't so bad, but with him they sent 'Buttercup' Fox."

"Maynard?"

"Yeah. Maynard."

"So now you have his quarters to yourself—"

"Great."

"—and you can get some sleep for a change. You've been complaining about that."

"Hell. Now he's got *me* reading at night, those damn silly Wild West books he reads."

"Well, at least a penny-dreadful can't shoot you," she said complacently.

"How's the hero doing?"

"Oh, wonderful," gushed Cassie. "He's been saying things. I think he comes from a big, wealthy family."

"Is that so? Not a bad-looking gent. That's a nasty cut, though. Who shaved him, you?"

"Maggie did."

"Cohen must've done something to make her mad."

"It was an accident, Clay."

"Sure, sure."

A good distance north of Outpost Number Nine, three riders rode down into a draw and back up out of it. Then they rode down into another, but when they came out of that one a bit later, they were leading three people afoot—medium, short, and small.

"You kids start walking," said one of the riders, and Elean-ora, Matthew, and Enos began to trudge back toward the wagon train from which they'd tried to escape.

Once they were back, Hiram McClellan made a statement.

"A while back, as you all might have noticed, a rider crossed our trail . . . a rider wearing the flowing black garb of death and pestilence. . . ."

This made his audience wonder a bit. They themselves wore flowing black or gray raiment.

"Yea, Satan at his most evil often assumes the clothes and

guise of the righteous, the better to insinuate himself among them. And thus it was with this rider, who clearly encouraged these children, Satan's children, to try to escape and join his loathesome followers. . . ."

"That ain't true!" cried Eleanora. "We was just lookin' for some friends."

"Silence!" thundered McClellan. "You have no friends among the living and good. We are the living and the good." He wiped his brow, which was moist with perspiration. "Out there is evil. Look about you. For one short moment we made contact with those people, and witness God's punishment. He is teaching us a lesson with these ills. No, there are no *friends* out there, only enemies. . . .

"But, to recall that rider, it is fortunate for us that he crossed our backtrail and not that before us. It was a warning, and we must heed that warning. Therefore we must change course.

Note that gap in the ridge to the northwest—Cutter's Gap— we will turn and go that way."

Sage nods met his announcement.

"As for the children, Satan clearly has them still firmly in his bondage. We must therefore keep them secure until we receive a sign from the Lord that they have been freed."

The wagon train turned northwest, heading for the distant gap, and Eleanora, Matthew, and Enos were bound and placed flat on the floor of the last wagon. Their companions in the wagon were still the same elders, who were now feeling even more poorly.

eight ─────────────────────

Matt Kincaid drove his men east across the prairie at a steady lope. After seeing the condition of Amy Selby's horse, a strong, fit, game animal, he knew better than to try to make it at a dead run as she had. He just hoped that Mallory, a man with whom he'd had a few pleasant pints, and Lieutenant Marlowe, to whom he'd quickly taken, would still be alive by the time they got there.

Windy rode ahead of the column, careful to keep himself a couple hundred yards ahead but not much more, unless he saw something.

Sergeant Olsen rode next to Kincaid, at the head of the first squad of First Platoon, followed by two corporals, the two-stripe squad leader, Miller, and one-stripe Lance Corporal Weatherby. Then came Malone and Dobbs, Holzer and Rottweiler, Parker and Medwick, Felson and Carter. Lieutenant Fox found himself bringing up the rear of the squad.

Lieutenant Fox reflected upon the fact that Indian chiefs often brought up the rear of their columns and, on further

69

reflection, considering the possibility of ambush, he didn't mind being back there.

Besides, if he were riding up front with Kincaid and Olsen, they'd both be trying to give him bits of tactical wisdom that he wouldn't know what to do with. He'd hoped for a posting to Florida, or the Carolinas, or his home state of New Hampshire, *anywhere* but out on the hostile frontier. Reading about it was as close as he'd ever wanted to get. But now that he was here . . .

He sighed. That fast-draw practice had been Smaldoon's idea, Smaldoon who, unless he was mistaken, had lately taken to calling him "Buttercup." He might have to take Mr. Smaldoon out behind the woodshed, so to speak.

Fox was a patient, easygoing, tolerant young man. But once he'd had enough, he did something about it. In his first year at the Point, as a young country gentleman from the southern part of New Hampshire, he'd taken considerable ribbing for his gentlemanly manner, his delicate ways, and his light, braying laugh. When he'd objected, he'd also taken several poundings.

He'd immediately set about rectifying the situation, on the sly hiring a hard-nosed Welsh boxer to teach him how to box. By the time he'd received his commission, his bray was a manly guffaw and he'd pounded the crap out of all that had pounded him, and done it several times for good measure.

Buttercup indeed.

"Ain't we gonna stay with them, sir?" asked Corporal Wilson, directly behind him.

Fox looked up, startled. In his reverie he'd let the first squad draw out ahead. "No sense bunching too tight," said Mister Fox, but then he urged his horse forward.

Kincaid heard the noise and turned to watch Mr. Fox charging forward. He sighed. *Damn dreamer, that Fox.* He said to Olsen, "When the action gets hot, *if* it does, try to keep an eye on Mr. Fox."

"Not if he's planning to shoot *my* toes off," said Olsen, grinning.

A couple of ranks back, Dobbs was still complaining to Malone. "Aw, hell, Malone, all she had was a bad case of pimples."

"I *told* you what she had, or probably had. Besides, you got stuck with that disease before, remember? Doctor had to slip that mercury up yer pecker. 'Member?"

"But the one I got that from didn't look the same as this."

"'Cause this one was *worse*."

"How the hell do you know?"

"'Cause Malone's mother had it when he was *born*." This comment came from right behind them, from Private Rottweiler. "How do you think he got to look like that?"

"Dizz-gusting," pronounced the other half of that German pair, Private Holzer, who'd got off the boat and joined the army under the impression he was signing up to homestead a quarter section. There was something about the English language he still hadn't quite got the hang of, but he was improving.

Malone, for his part, showed quite a bit of forbearance for one so handy with his fists. It may have been the proximity of the first officer or the unavailability of intoxicating fluids. "Yep, I do, I got me looks straight from me ma. But Rottweiler... he got his from his *dog*." Malone started cackling like crazy.

"Hold it down, Private," ordered Kincaid. "You're waking up the whole territory. *Nobody* can stand a laugh like that."

There wasn't any snapping back at the first officer, so instead Malone twisted in his saddle and asked quietly, "How come everything blew up over there, anybody know?"

"Understand the missionaries and the Sanitary Corps started fightin' over the Cheyenne," said Parker. "And the Cheyenne got pissed."

"You're kiddin'."

Parker shrugged. "That's what I hear. Someone got their signals crossed."

"I don't blame Mr. Lo," said Malone reasonably. "Them missionaries can be a pain in the butt. I'm Catholic. I *know* about them bastards."

"They're Presbyterians," said Medwick.

"Same thing," said Malone. "They'll all kill you for your soul."

"And I heard the Sanitary Corps was tryin' to vaccinate them 'gainst smallpox."

Malone started sputtering. "*Vaccinate*? With them *needles*? No wonder..."

"Cheyenne's got *lances* what ain't as long as them needles," said Stretch.

"Bull," said Rottweiler. "Needle ain't no longer'n yer pecker, Stretch."

Dobbs saw his opportunity. "That's what I just said," he boasted.

They started cackling again.

"I *said* hold it down."

"Hell," whispered Malone, "horses are fartin' louder'n we're laughin'."

"Injuns don't pay no 'tention to farts," claimed Medwick. "An' talk about evil *smells*. Which reminds me, I also heard the Sanitaries was trying to teach the Cheyenne to crap in a latrine."

Malone frowned. "How the hell do you do that? Hold 'em down and *spoon* it out?"

"Dizzz-*gusting*!" cried Wolfgang Holzer.

"Holzer!" spat Matt, twisting around quickly. "I'm about to blow your head off."

"Hey, sir, what do you think?" asked Malone.

"About what?"

"'Bout the missionaries and the Sanitary Corps?"

"Well," said Matt, "they've got to be vaccinated, or else there might not be any left."

"That's bad?" muttered Parker.

"But as for the missionaries converting, and the crapping in latrines..." Matt shook his head slowly.

"Hey, Malone," said Medwick. "You know so much about missionaries—you see that missionary gal ride in?"

"*Did* I? Hey, I wouldn't mind converting...uh-oh, here comes Windy."

Sure enough, Windy Mandalian was riding toward them.

Matt halted the column as Windy arrived. "What's up? We're nowhere near the agency yet."

"I know. But there are fresh horse turds up ahead, and they ain't army."

Matt thought aloud. "Cheyenne patrol, figured we'd be coming, came out to watch for us. Then what? Headed back or hid?"

"Hid, likely," said Sergeant Olsen, and Matt paid attention; Olsen was one it paid to listen to. "Don't figure they came out jes' to make sure we was comin', they'd know that soon enough. More likely to slow us up, give the rest a chance to either bring up braves or clear the hell out."

"All right," said Matt, "I hate doing it because we're so far away, but...spread 'em out Sergeant, spread out the first squad—"

"Shit," muttered Parker.

"Hold the second and third back in reserve, second on the right, third on the left. Mr. Fox, why don't you command the right side there. Take Olsen with you. Windy, you stick with me." And Matt began to angle off to the left with Windy and part of the first squad.

They rode forward until they reached the point where Windy had found the turds. There they paused and Matt looked over the terrain up ahead.

About a quarter-mile distant was a rise in the land with a notch in it, just about dead ahead, through which one would normally ride. Undoubtedly that was where the attack would come, if it came.

They dismounted and advanced slowly, spread out, their horses trailing on long leads.

They hadn't quite halved the distance when suddenly they began taking fire. All three squads hit the ground, but just the first returned the fire.

The exchange was heavy but brief, the fire from the Cheyenne side suddenly quitting. There was a pause, and then three Cheyenne braves rode up out of a draw and headed for the notch in the distant rise.

"Damn repeaters," swore Malone. "I thought there was more."

"There are," said Windy as he and Matt and the rest leaped aboard their horses and took out after the Cheyenne. Matt and Sergeant Olsen, riding at the head of their men, exchanged looks and nods.

The retreating Cheyenne vanished through the gap.

Immediately the pursuing force split, Matt taking part of the first squad and the entire third to the left, Olsen leading Fox and the rest to the right.

The platoon, thus split, then drove their horses at the steeper incline flanking the notch. If Matt and Olsen had guessed right, the Cheyenne had pulled this trick once too often.

And they *had* guessed right. Topping the rise, they looked down and saw about thirty Cheyenne waiting in ambush on both sides of the trail through the notch.

Matt and the platoon hit the ground, falling to comfortable firing positions, and started blasting away.

But the Cheyenne sensed that something was amiss and, with the first shots, realized they'd been outmaneuvered. They lost no time in getting away, mounting their ponies on the dead run. Only eight Cheyenne were left behind to feed the prairie.

Matt and his men mounted and gave chase, but soon discovered that the Cheyenne weren't through fighting. No sooner had the twenty-odd remaining Cheyenne gotten out of rifle range than they dismounted and waited for Matt and his platoon to ride closer, at which time they opened fire. Matt and the platoon had to hit the ground and return the fire, whereupon the Cheyenne leaped aboard their ponies and pulled back out of range. And then Matt and the boys remounted and took off after them. And then the entire routine was repeated.

It was a damned slow way to ride to the rescue, thought Matt. Tiring, too—mounting, dismounting, crawling, then mounting, dismounting, crawling. He wasn't losing any men, but neither were the Cheyenne. And in the meantime the agency was getting shot up.

After the third repetition, Matt called Fox and Olsen over. "Mr. Fox, take Olsen and the second squad and keep on playing this game. I'll take the rest and ride around them."

Fox nodded and Olsen said, "Go get 'em, sir. We'll keep these fellas busy."

The platoon rode forward as before, but when they saw the Cheyenne dismounting and they started taking fire, Matt and Windy swung the first and third squads sharply to the right and began to ride like hell.

The Cheyenne didn't realize what was happening until Matt began to bend his men around their flank, but when they did catch on, they realized they'd already been outflanked and started to take up positions that protect their front and rear.

Let them, thought Matt, failing to complete the circle but instead, following Windy, straightening out and making a beeline for the agency. Matt was tempted to leave a squad, or part of one, behind to finish off the surrounded hostiles, but he didn't want to weaken himself when he didn't know exactly what kind of fight he was riding into.

When he did reach the reservation and the agency, he wished he had left the squad. The fight was over, the entire Cheyenne village having decamped, and Mallory was standing outside the agency as Matt and his men rode up.

"Guessed you were coming," said Mallory. "They had us dead to rights, but they suddenly picked up and skedaddled. The girl get through?"

"Yep," said Matt, scanning the area.

"And Forrest?"

Matt saw missionaries and members of the Sanitary Corps picking through the dead and wounded, both white and Cheyenne. "Just her," he finally said. "Who's Forrest?"

"Took a ton of lead getting out with her. Hoped he might last."

"Marlowe?"

"He's fine." Mallory suddenly grinned. "Madder'n hell that the Cheyenne got repeaters while we only had single-shot."

"The good Dr. Marlowe?"

"The good Dr. Marlowe," said Marlowe, coming up behind Matt, "was busy counting plenty coups, as I believe the expression goes. And I would have counted a damn sight more with a decent rifle that didn't take eternity to reload."

"Shoot 'em up and then patch 'em up," said Mallory, grinning. "That's Doc Marlowe."

But Matt was shaking his head sadly. "Sorry, Doc, but you've got to touch them with something held in your hand to earn a coup."

"I was. I was holding the rifle."

"But you weren't holding the bullet."

"I think you're being a bit too demanding," sniffed Marlowe.

"Bet you're glad you're alive," Matt said.

"You're goddamn right I am."

"We all are, Matt," said Mallory. "It got nasty."

"How many'd we lose?"

"Missionaries lost three or four. Corps lost Billingsgate and a couple of privates that kicked the whole thing off, near as I can determine . . . and another private back here, trying to get to the agency. And there's a whole crew missing—a doctor, two assistants, and seven privates, latrine-diggers mostly. If they got *them*, figure fifteen, give or take a few."

Matt whistled softly.

"Would that rate as a massacre?" Mallory asked.

"Your sense of humor is sometimes in poor taste," Matt said. "How'd it start?"

Marlowe took a deep breath. "Two privates were trying to wrestle a Cheyenne into one of the latrines," he said dully. "Missionaries were trying to convince the Cheyenne that there was a hell under the ground, the Corps was stabbing them with needles, and apparently the Cheyenne figured that the latrines, the holes in the ground, were just a faster way of getting them down to hell. . . ."

There were some more opinions offered, mostly similar and understanding if unavoidably bitter, which Matt considered. "Well, then," he finally concluded, "it's more a tragic misunderstanding and the Cheyenne thinking they had to defend themselves than a real outbreak of hostilities."

"I dunno," muttered Mallory. "Hostilities broke out pretty good around here."

"You know what I mean."

"Yeah, I do. And lucky I'm so understanding. And lucky for the Cheyenne it's you here instead of some fire-eater. I know some soldiers that'd be out to kill every Indian they seen. But you just can't blame the Cheyenne for not being white and Christian and tolerant toward being stabbed with needles."

Just then a Sanitary Corps private rode up to say he thought he'd found the missing crew.

They all rode over to the other side of the Cheyenne village—or where it used to be—to the partially filled latrine pit.

"Well, where are they?" asked Marlowe.

"Down there. That pit was dug out complete. I think they're buried."

"Oh, God."

Just then they heard a moan, or thought they did. They looked around for the source and couldn't find any. Then they heard it again.

"It's coming from down there. Someone's buried alive."

Matt, Marlowe, Mallory, and two soldiers immediately leaped into the pit and started digging with their hands. Another soldier rode for help and shovels.

By the time the shovels and willing workers got there, the top layer of corpses had been partially uncovered, still bristling with syringes.

Ten minutes later the two living privates had been dragged from the bottom of the pile, nearly suffocated. Fortunately for them, the tangle of bodies had provided just enough pockets of air to last until then.

At about that time, Privates Malone and Dobbs were wandering through another part of the village grounds, checking out the sod huts. "Don't look like no one lived in them," said Malone, coming out of one.

"Hey," said Dobbs, "ain't that a funny place for a scarecrow? There ain't nothin' planted around here."

They walked the distance to the scarecrow, slowing as they got closer.

"Oh, shit," said Malone.

It was one of the Black Robes. He had been mutilated by countless coups and hung out in a grotesque parody of the Crucifixion, an act in which the Black Robes, for some reason completely incomprehensible to the Cheyenne, found cause for celebration.

Malone and Dobbs took the poor man down from his cross.

A few hours later the missionaries and the Sanitary Corps began the slow trek back to Outpost Number Nine with the dead and wounded. And Matt assembled his platoon preparatory to taking off after the Cheyenne.

Fox and Olsen had shown up with the second squad. They'd routed the Cheyenne, killing five and watching the rest race off to the north.

Olsen also reported having found Private Forrest.

"Son of a bitch was still alive. Five or six bullet holes, an' a goddamn dent in his head, an' unconscious. He took a whole passel out, the girl wouldn't have made it otherwise. Met the wagons out yonder just a little bit, gave 'im to Doc Marlowe."

"He'll live?"

Olsen shrugged. "Dunno. Ol' Marlowe already worked one miracle with that bounty man."

Matt nodded, then said, "Sent a rider back to get some men headed north. Windy figures the Cheyenne are heading for the mountains."

"Which ones?"

"Big Horns. Wind River. If they get there, it'll be hard to catch 'em. But they've got some distance to go before they get to 'em. Windy figures they'll head for Cutter's Gap. The men heading north will try to keep them from getting there, but if they don't, there should be another bunch coming up the other side of that ridge, to catch 'em coming out or somehow keep them from getting too far west. Hell, a whole damn village can't move all *that* fast."

"Are we riding through the night?"

"Nope. Horses can't take it, even if the men could. We'll have to go a ways, then bivouac and hope they stop too, though their ponies are a hell of a lot fresher than our mounts. Anyhow, I don't think it calls for a big fight." He explained how the hostilities had begun. "I'd like to tread kind of easy, stay in touch, keep 'em moving in circles, sort of herd them around. They'll get tired sooner or later, and when they see we're not determined to kill 'em, they'll give up."

"Maybe," said Olsen.

"Let's hope," said Matt. There's good killing and there's bad. All this around here was bad."

nine

"Lemme tell you, Arnold," said Jeff Dow, private and short-timer in the Army of the West, "this Bennett woman—Giselle Bennett, you remember her?—well, she may be sweet but she sure ain't shy. But hell, *you* gotta know *that*. . . .

"Now this here homestead, this is about as pretty a deal as a man'd care to fall into, but I don't know if I'm ready to settle for just one woman. Man like me don't have no trouble findin' women. An' *farmin'*? Hell, I joined the army just to get away from the damn farm, whaddya think of *that*? I know, I know, Zelly thinks I love her, an' I don't blame her, an' she's got a nice body for a gal her age. She ever tell *you* how old she was? Prob'ly did. Hell, you knew her when she *was* young. But Naomi, there's"—he looked around to make sure he wasn't being overheard—"there's a real good reason for gettin' hitched. Set around waitin' for *that* young thing to come of age. That's if she ain't of age already. You seen her recent? Guess you have, can't help it. Come *on*, Arnold, don't look like that. So she's young. So what? I'm young too, younger'n

Zelly anyway. An' Naomi, she's about ready to be broken in. Who better but yours truly to do the dirty deed? Gotta be done *some* time. 'Course, like as not I'll be all set and Zelly'll have me cleanin' out chickenshit or sloppin' the hawgs or some damn thing. For such a sweet-lookin' filly, she sure can think of some dirty jobs for me to do...."

He scratched his head and watched a distant rider. Looked like an army rider, and riding like hell.

"And then again, ol' Sergeant Cohen's been after me hot 'n heavy to re-up. B'sides gettin' new men, the army's gotta keep the ones they got. Ol' Rutherford figures he'll *crowd* Mr. Lo out with soldiers. I been givin' Cohen the runaround recent, but I gotta tell 'im yes or no real soon...."

"Who're you talking to, Jeff?"

Jeff Dow whirled around. Naomi Bennett was there, having snuck up on him and caught him deep in conversation with Mr. Arnold Bennett, the scarecrow.

"I was jes' talkin' with the scarecrow here, rehearsin' my farewell speech to the army."

Naomi grinned at him, wrapping her arms tightly around her chest, just under and pushing her healthy young breasts up and out. They about burst from her blouse. Jeff prayed a couple of buttons would let go. But hell, they'd better not or else he'd be all over her then and there, with the unsuspecting Zelly Bennett barely a shotgun blast away. And she could handle that damn thing.

But the way Naomi smiled, the way her light brown hair fell and broke softly over her shoulders, those green, laughing eyes....

"What are you looking at, Jeff? Have I got something dirty on me?"

"Oh, no, *no*...."

"Who was that rider, d'you think?"

"Army. Headin' for the post. Might be somethin' goin' on. Which means I better get back."

"Oh, noooo...."

"Sorry, kid." Boy, he loved the way she hated to see him go; she was going to be a pushover. "Duty calls."

She chewed on a knuckle and looked at him mischievously? "But not for long, right Jeff?"

"Right you are, sweetheart. Now come on." He walked up beside her, turned her around, and gave her a friendly pat on her compact butt. "I gotta say goodbye to Zelly."

She threw an arm around him and squeezed. He felt real good.

The messenger from Kincaid, Private Fritsch from the third squad, came off his horse in front of the orderly room and hit the ground running, liking the effect it made. He pounded into the orderly room and made his report.

"Well," said Captain Conway after Fritsch was gone, "it's Smaldoon's turn to go out, but dammit, Clay's not the type for a herding operation. And I think Matt's got the right idea on that. But I guess I'll have to send both out anyway, one up the east slope, one up the west. Hell, might as well send them both at the same time."

"Sergeant Breckenridge can probably hold Mr. Smaldoon down, sir," said Sergeant Cohen. "I think Breckenridge could probably have kept Napoleon outa Roosha."

"Mmm, probably so. If I remember rightly, Sergeant Breckenridge's spoken sharply to *me* a couple of times."

"I'm sure you're mistaken, sir," said Cohen diplomatically, trying to make sure his good sergeants stayed sergeants. "I'll send for Smaldoon and Allison."

Five minutes later the runner was back with the news that Lieutenant Smaldoon was, for the moment, mysteriously incapacitated. Captain Conway decided to see for himself what this mysterious incapacitation was. He marched from the orderly room.

But no sooner had he hit the parade then he saw the door to Fox's quarters open and Smaldoon emerge, quick-stepping toward the nearest latrine. Smaldoon caught sight of Captain Conway and threw him a weak salute, but didn't slow up.

Captain Conway went back to the orderly room. "Smaldoon has the runs," he told Cohen, fighting to keep a grin off his face. "I hope Allison's all right."

Mr. Smaldoon was back in Fox's quarters, waiting despondently for the next attack.

The door opened and Mr. Allison, dressed for battle, stuck his head in. "Heard you were sick, Clay."

"I'm not sick," snorted Smaldoon. "I've got the runs. That stuff that Amy Breckenridge fixed last night did me in. Didn't you have any?" His mood was dark and thunderous. "Damn. Made me miss a chance to get some hostiles. And here I have to sit, in Fox's quarters, while some damn bounty hunter's using *my* bed. Goddammit, it's not fair. I'm an *officer*."

Mr. Allison tried to look sympathetic. Then his eyes suddenly widened and he had to stand clear as Smaldoon charged by on his way to the latrine.

But just a little while later Smaldoon was there again, smoldering away in Fox's quarters. He was wondering if he shouldn't just stay in the latrine. He knew the men were laughing at him—the officers, the noncoms, and the enlistees. Damn.

Maybe there was a chamber pot or something he could use. He could dump it when it got dark.

The door opened again and Cassie Smaldoon entered.

"Heard you were sick, Clay."

"I am. But I'm surprised you could tear yourself away from that bounty man."

"Oh, Clay. Be reasonable."

"Yeah, sure . . . only good thing is that there's hardly anything left to come out of me."

"Oh, you're sick *that* way."

"Didn't you know? Isn't it all over the post?"

"All over the post? Haven't you been using the latrine?"

Smaldoon suddenly started laughing.

In the Smaldoon quarters, the wounded man came awake. He lay there for a second, eyes wide open, steady, and clear. He seemed suddenly and miraculously possessed of total awareness. But the fact was that he'd awakened briefly at other times, usually during the night, and his brain had had time to clear.

He sat up now, slowly, feeling stiffness, lingering pain, and tight bandages around his midsection. He inspected the bandages and concluded from their extent that it had been a bad wound.

He peeked under the bandages, lost count of the stitches, saw the puckered skin healing nicely, and wondered who the doc had been. The wound should have killed him. He'd killed enough men himself with gutshots. It was slow but pretty certain. The doc had been good.

He also wondered who his nurse was. He'd seen her shape only at night, when it was dark.

He swung his legs off the bed and stood up. He was suddenly

dizzy, but willed himself steady. Slowly he walked to the window and looked out.

Well, what do you know, an army post.

He turned away and started walking around the room, glancing out the window each time he went by, to make sure no one surprised him.

He felt himself walking more steadily. Hell, he'd always been a fast healer. The good life, he thought mockingly, that's what did it.

Rachel, he suddenly remembered. His sister and her children. His face hardened and he began to walk faster, harder, pushing himself, alive again with purpose.

By the time Cassie Smaldoon returned, he'd tired himself out and was back in bed, eyes closed. He peeked at Cassie in the light and saw a good-looking woman. Then another woman appeared, bearing a pile of cloth. "Hello, Maggie," said the younger woman to the older newcomer. Then she said to him, "Time to have your bandages changed, Mr. Bounty Hunter...and maybe Maggie can shave you again without cutting you to death."

The wounded man, seemingly unconscious, almost gave a start.

Meanwhile, Lieutenant Allison and Sergeant Chubb had formed up the second and third squads from the Third Platoon. They didn't take the full platoon since more men had to be sent west of Cutter's Gap, and when *they* left, the post would be dangerously undermanned if a squad or two hadn't been left behind.

Amos Fletcher and his mangy bunch, lounging around outside the sutler's, watched the men mount up and prepare to leave.

"Dang it, Reb," said Amos, "iffen thet payroll would only come now, it'd be perfect. There wouldn't be no one left to chase us."

"Yeah, yeah, yeah," said Reb, dropping the bottle from his lips and drooling down the front of his shirt.

Pop Evans, the sutler, came out of his store, took a look at Reb, and turned and went back in.

Private Dow rode in just as Allison and his men rode out. "Hey, that's *my* platoon," he protested.

"Your platoon, soldier," said Sergeant Cohen, who happened to be standing near the main gate, going over guard strength with Corporal Hicks, corporal of the new guard, "but it ain't your squad. Your squad stayed behind. In fact, your squad's pulling guard. Go draw yourself a weapon and report to Corporal Hicks here."

"Aw, hell, Sarge. How come I can't do no fightin'?"

"For one thing, like I said, *your* squad's pullin' guard. And for another, you're too short. Won't send you till I have to, unless...unless you'd care to put your John Hancock on the dotted line and re-up for three more years."

Private Dow grinned. "Jes' because you know I'm a good fighter, you think you got me. But I'll tell you, Sarge, I'm also a good lover, and I got me a woman. . . ." His grin, widening, completed the sentence.

Cohen shook his head. That wasn't any reason, he thought. A man could be a soldier and still have a woman. But he knew the woman was the widow Bennett, and that she needed a full-time man. Buy why Dow? He was fair as a soldier, sometimes good, but that was about all he was good for, as far as Cohen could see.

Corporal Hicks, for his part, greeted Dow's boast that he was a good lover with a groan. He and the rest of the first squad, Enright in particular, sometimes found Dow hard to take. The common run of men in the Army of the West weren't gems, he knew that, but Dow was sometimes a little dumber and rougher than most. This widow Bennett he'd hooked up with had to be a real loser.

"Hell," groaned Dow, "this post'll have to be attacked before I see any more action."

"You want some action?" growled Lance Corporal Enright, coming up, and Dow didn't like the sound of that. "Don't complain, you've had it made. And what're you just standing around for? Put that horse up and get your tail back over here."

"Who made *you* boss?"

"*I* made me boss," said Enright, also known as Ironfist, and Dow sullenly led his horse away.

"Wagons approaching!" came a cry from the guard atop the tower.

Cohen came out of the orderly room wondering if these were the wagons from the agency. If so, they sure made good time.

Amos Fletcher and his crowd stared at each other in consternation. "The payroll!" croaked Amos hoarsely, and he and his gang began to drift around the parade, subtly taking up positions. They'd foreseen that this might happen.

Of course, it was insane to think that they could take the payroll, right there in the middle of Outpost Number Nine, with some forty to fifty soldiers still hanging around. But they'd passed beyond the pale as far as clear, sane thinking was concerned.

Sergeant Breckenridge, hunkered down in front of the enlisted barracks, in the afternoon shade, saw them spreading out and his gut started to tighten. He, too, thought it might be the paymaster rolling in.

But it wasn't. It was, instead, an eighteen-wagon train hauled by six teams of ten bull oxen each. The train brought the supplies for the post—mountains of grain for the horses, tins and sacks and packages of food for the men, and ammo and gun replacements for Ordnance, to mention just the essentials. But they also brought some light gear for Skinflint Wilson, who doubled as both Supply and Ordnance, and miscellaneous items, anything specially ordered, and supplies for the sutler.

Cohen, with his sergeants from the mess and Supply, went through, checking off items. Sergeant Breckenridge had formed up Second Platoon to see to the unloading. He was still keeping an eye on the mangy bunch, but he'd relaxed some as Amos began to draw his people back together again outside the sutler's.

"Shoulda known it wasn't the payroll," groused Fletcher. "We woulda got word if it was comin'."

"You sure thet brother of yers is ree-liable?"

"Yep. He knows if he ain't he'll be seein' me again, and he don't want that. He'll send the message."

"Just as well," said a slack-faced youngster. "We woulda got our asses shot off, sure as anything," and he took to cackling.

The rest grinned inanely along with him, agreeing that that would have been the case. Sure would have been some big shootout.

"But don't you fret, chillun," said Amos soothingly, "it's all gonna come our way soon enough."

ten

Hiram McClellan and his wagon train had spent the night within a few hours' drive of Cutter's Gap. They figured they'd go through in the morning.

Hiram had seen no more riders, no evil omens, and his heart was full and glad, even though he himself felt awful, physically.

Another child had died in the night. Many more, young and old, were barely able to sit upright; most, in fact, were lying down while the strongest drove the wagons.

Thinking about it, Hiram's heart was less full and less glad. How had they offended God to be punished in such a manner? After all, if God had not intended that they make contact with those strangers, the ones that had fixed the wheels, would He have caused the wheels to break?

Truly, He moved in mysterious ways. It had been a test, and in some obscure way that Hiram did not yet understand, they had failed.

It was light in the east now, and Hiram, lying beneath the lead wagon, crawled out and got to his feet. He could hear weeping. The child had died at the darkest hour of the night. Hiram had arisen and watched the spirit depart, led the prayers, and then returned to merciful slumber. But the mother had begun to weep, and she wept still. She had two other children, and they too were ill. When would it end?

Hiram roused the rest of the wagon train, and through a discipline that surmounted their dreadful weakness, they began to move on.

They had not gone far when they saw that there was another large party converging on the same gap in the ridge. Hiram urged the wagon train on. If they hurried, they would get there first, go through ahead of the others, and avoid contact.

Chief Hungry Buffalo, leading the distant Cheyenne, the entire reservation village—some two hundred, including women and children—already knew of McClellan's wagon train. His scouts had told him of it and he'd ridden forward to see for himself. He judged that the wagons would reach the gap before his party did. Would the wagons then block the gap and wish to fight? Were the wagons full of American soldiers?

He too urged more speed from his people, many of whom walked, resting their own ponies and leading the other ponies that dragged travois. But his people were tired, especially the oldest. They'd traveled through the night, during which time the excitement had worn off. But they *had* to reach the mountains before the American soldiers caught up; there they would be safe.

But if the Americans did catch them, they'd have to fight. They would not go back to the Black Robes and the Long Needles. They would die first.

Chief Hungry Buffalo called four braves to his side and told them to find out who rode the wagons, to look especially for concealed blue-clad soldiers. The scouts rode off.

Hiram McClellan saw the scouts approaching, remote figures. But as they got closer he was able to see, despite his fever-clouded vision, that they were . . . shades of hell! They were painted *blue*!

He'd never seen nor heard of warpaint—which the Cheyenne, since the previous day's battle, had not bothered to remove—and did not see these Indians as human. These were clearly emissaries of the devil, and yonder people, silhouetted blackly against the skyline, moving wearily, were clearly travelers down the road to hell.

"Brethren! Arm yourselves! Satan attacks!" he roared.

The sick, enfeebled "brethren" managed to bestir themselves, and weapons poked from the wagons. And when the four braves came within range of those weapons, which were long rifles, ancient muzzle-loaders, long in length and range, they opened fire.

The four Cheyenne had thought they were safe, well beyond the range of the army Springfield or carbine, or anything save the buffalo gun, but when two of their number flung up their arms and pitched from their ponies, they knew that they were not. The two remaining braves spun their mounts and hightailed it back toward Chief Hungry Buffalo and the rest of the Cheyenne.

But Hungry Buffalo did not need to wait for them to arrive to know what had happened. He'd seen the braves fall and then heard the shots. He'd called to his warriors, and without a second's delay, he sent them raining down upon McClellan's ill-fated wagon train.

Lieutenant Allison, leaving the previous afternoon, had led his men north, heading for the eastern side of Cutter's Gap. He'd set a fast pace but, like Matt, not so fast as to exhaust their mounts. All they'd need was to suddenly come upon the hostiles and have to take temporary evasive action on tired horses.

Platoon Sergeant Chubb rode beside him. They were a good pair—Mr. Allison serious and reserved, Sergeant Chubb laconic by nature. Both had sharp minds, albeit differently trained, Allison's by education, Chubb's by experience.

Both were tall, lanky men, Chubb's frame belying his name. Their faces were different, though, as different as their backgrounds. Chubb's was angular, slightly coarse, but considerably leavened by humorous brown eyes and a generous, expressive mouth. Allison's was long and refined.

Allison looked into the distance. He could see the beginnings of the ridge, along the eastern slope of which they'd soon be riding. "Where do you suppose Robert is?"

Robert was their Delaware scout, originally named, rather awkwardly, Tree That Grows Long and Tall. The Delaware had lived so long with the white man that he'd thought to assume a "white" name, which he did—Robert Longtrees.

Scouts for the Army of the West were frequently Delaware, an Eastern tribe pushed west from the Jersey area but unable to set up shop as a powerful Plains tribe. Thus they tended to hook up with the army. And in their favor was the fact they spoke Algonquin, or at least a version of that language, which was the linguistic coin of the realm of the Plains.

"He's out there somewhere," answered Chubb. "But don't worry," he added with a wry smile. "Robert don't ever get too far ahead."

"How much longer do you think it will take?"

"Plannin' to ride through the night, sir?"

"Wouldn't you, if you were hoping to head off Mr. Lo?"

"'Long about midmornin', the men'll be red-eyed and tired 'bout then. Sight of some hostiles'll perk 'em right up, though. That's if them hostiles're dumb enough to sleep."

"What do you mean, Sergeant?"

"I mean if they ride right through, travelin' village or not, they'll beat us to the pass."

"We should ride faster?"

"And end up on foot?"

"That was my thinking."

"But prepare yourself to hear some grumblin' from the men 'long about two in the mornin'."

"Poor dears," muttered Allison, and Chubb smiled.

As night fell that same previous day, back at Outpost Number Nine, Captain Conway was venting his displeasure. "Smaldoon hasn't eaten anything for twenty-four hours, not since Amy poisoned him. How come it's still coming out?"

Sergeant Cohen, sitting at his desk, watching Captain Conway pace back and forth, said glumly, "Ain't comin' out solid." He'd never been at ease with anything to do with toilets, humorous or otherwise. "Drank a lot of water, for the fever."

"Could it be cholera?"

"Nope," Cohen replied. "Fever's gone. Should be fit by mornin'."

"He should have left by now. If the Cheyenne beat Allison to Cutter's Gap and get through, we should have someone up the other side to cut them off. I'd go myself, except that would leave Smaldoon in charge, and I have visions of some kind of mutiny."

"Smaldoon ain't like that, sir."

Conway's silence grudgingly conceded the point. But at the same time, Smaldoon wasn't a Point man, nor was he from any other kind of military school.

"You looked in on your wife recently, sir?" asked Cohen, to distract him.

Captain Conway appreciated that Cohen not only looked after his men but his officers. And just then he was looking after Conway's temper. It would be hard to get through a day without Sergeant Cohen. "No," he said, "but she and Maggie and some of the girls are supposed to be busy exchanging some of *our* money over a friendly game of cards."

"Amy Breckenridge ain't friendly when it comes to cards."

"I know. Sergeant Breckenridge will probably soon retire on our money. Flora's probably wagering my retirement wages right now. Lucky we don't own the deed to anything. Of course, if ol' Rutherford 'Tightwad' Hayes doesn't lift the freeze on promotions, and I never get beyond captain, that retirement money won't amount to a hill of beans. That's if I can ever *afford* to retire."

Just then the orderly room door opened. Mr. Smaldoon entered in full battle dress, which meant simply that, aside from his usual post garb, he was wearing his wide-brimmed campaign hat and was sporting both guns, the Scoff and the hair-trigger S&W.

Conway eyed him, slightly puzzled. "I can handle OD, Clay, you don't have to push yourself." But the campaign hat continued to bother him.

"I ain't ready for OD, sir. I'm ready to ride."

"You're . . . ummmm . . . dried up?"

"Last time I felt the urge, I found I could hold it in. I'm ready, sir."

Captain Conway glanced at Sergeant Cohen, who said, "Maybe an early call tomor—"

But Captain Conway cut in, his mind made up, "Roust Sergeant Breckenridge."

"Aw, hell, sir," said Breckenridge from the door, "I'm already rousted. Mr. Smaldoon here done that little favor. I was dead to the world, too."

"You were already asleep?" wondered Captain Conway.

"Shore was, sir. Gotta be bright-eyed in th' mornin' t' figure what to do with all thet money Amy's winnin'."

Captain Conway's mouth opened and closed several times,

but no words emerged, just noises.

"And the second and third squads have been told," Breckenridge went on. "They're jes' settin' around waitin' t' hear the good news, one of them lovely moonlight rides."

"Right you are, Sergeant," snapped Conway. "A moonlight ride. Move them out, west side of Cutter's Gap. And Mr. Smaldoon . . . we're out to round them up, not decimate them. You *do* appreciate the difference?"

"Yessir. It's time to play games with the hostiles."

"Not games. Justice."

"Don't worry, sir. If I tried to do differently, I'd have Breck all over me."

"You'd like to have a different sergeant?" inquired Captain Conway.

"No, sir, they're all the same in this company. Same way *I* used to be. Couldn't trust an officer to even wipe his own nose correct." He turned to Breckenridge. "Let's go, Sarge, go play nursemaid."

They rode out twenty minutes later, in the dead of night, a full two squads, plus Breckenridge and Smaldoon. *Plus* another Delaware scout, this one named Peter. Just Peter. No one knew what his true name had been.

Along about ten the next morning, Allison and his men rode north along the eastern slope of the ridge. They peered into the distance and saw buzzards circling, swarms of buzzards.

Chubb spoke for them all. "Either Matt caught up with them, or they run into some poor bastards. Going by the number of them birds, some sizeable bunch of bastards. Maybe they got the taste of blood, and liked it. Hell, they always *did* like to fight."

True enough, thought Allison. The Cheyenne were as fierce a collection of fighters as ever gathered on the northern Plains.

Without any signal, the entire troop began to ride faster.

A half-hour later they were picking through the bloody remains of Hiram McClellan's wagon train. Everyone was dead, scalped and mutilated. There were two oddities though: no fingers had been cut off, and a few were found that didn't have a killing mark on them.

"While most of the corpses are still warm, sir," said Private Palmatier of the third squad, "or they ain't real cold, these here are icier'n January. Must've died well ahead of the rest. Couldn't even pry their scalps off, or didn't try hard enough. And one, hid in a wagon, ain't got a mark on him. Jes' a little feller too."

But before Allison and Chubb could interpret that one, there came a shout: "Riders!"

They looked to the west automatically, guts tightening, but saw nothing. Then they looked east and saw riders gathering on a nearby rise.

"It's Matt," said Chubb, as the distant riders kicked their horses into motion.

Five minutes later, Matt Kincaid and First Platoon were in among them, also looking over the McClellan wagon train massacre. Allison filled Matt, Lieutenant Fox, and Sergeant Olsen in on what he knew, including the two oddities.

Fox frowned and then plunged into the gore, aided by Private Palmatier. Matt was surprised.

Fox and Palmatier were still in there picking around, when another couple of privates, Shortsleeves (orginally Zschortas-levski) and Murdoch, rode in from the north, where they'd gone scouting with Robert. "They didn't go down empty, sir," said Shortsleeves. "They got themselves a number of them red bastards. A far piece out, too."

"That's because they were using some old guns, sir," said Lance Corporal Cameron, addressing both Matt and Mr. Allison. "Some old muskets, powder and ball, but in good shape and *long* ones, ol' Kentucky specials, shoot accurate as long, if not as heavy, as a Sharps."

They all nodded for a while. Then Allison said, "I wonder why it happened? The Cheyenne were supposed to be running. They weren't a war party. And the wagon train wouldn't have attacked *them*—these folk are dressed like some kind of pil-grims. Doesn't make all that much sense. Think the Cheyenne were still that feisty after riding the whole night? I know *I'm* tired enough not to look for trouble."

"You're not a Cheyenne," responded Matt, "and you never look for trouble anyway, but you're right, it doesn't make all that much sense."

The entire force was suddenly electrified by the cry, "We got some live ones!"

Lieutenants Kincaid and Allison, and Sergeants Chubb and Olsen rode toward the rear of the wagon train, where three people stood unsteadily next to the last wagon: Eleanora, Matthew and Enos Culloch.

There was wonder in Corporal Lowenstein's voice as he said, "They was bound hand and foot and was underneath a mess of dead bodies. Lucky Private Cox here don't mind wadin' through blood and guts, or we might not have found them for a while."

Cox, from the third squad of Allison's platoon, couldn't decide whether to look proud or not. Lowenstein's words made it sound like he'd wade through anything.

Eleanora and her brothers stood silently, overwhelmed by the appearance of these strange men in blue. She and her brothers had wanted to get away, to find friends, but these did not look all that friendly. Besides which, the recent horror was still fresh in their minds.

"You kids got names?" asked Matt.

They remained silent. Allison slowly dismounted and walked over to them. He swept off his hat, letting his blond hair fall lightly over his high forehead. His patrician features softened considerably. He reached out and tousled young Enos' hair and then drew the boy to him. After a moment's hesitation the young boy clung to Mr. Allison, tears flowing.

"The group was religious," said Mr. Allison an hour later, filling Kincaid, Olsen, and Chubb in on what he'd learned. Lieutenant Fox came up and joined them, a troubled expression on his face, soon after Allison had begun.

"Came from a part of Pennsylvania," said Allison, "as near as I could determine. Been isolated for years. I mean, for as long as Eleanora's been alive—she's nineteen—she's never seen a stranger. They may have been isolated for twenty, thirty, forty years—who knows?"

Allison went on to describe why the three youngsters had been bound, the details of the trip west including the broken wheels and contacts with people at Schuyler, the sickness, the messianic behavior of Hiram McClellan, and finally the battle.

"Cheyenne must have sent some scouts to look them over. All the kids know is that suddenly word was passed that Satan was upon them, and the men of the wagon train opened fire. They're clear about that. There wasn't any shooting before the menfolk opened up. They had those long rifles. Probably picked the scouts off back where the scouts thought they were safe.

After that the attack came. These kids were already bound up and lying in the last wagon. People fell on top of them and were scalped, but somehow the Cheyenne didn't notice them."

He finished.

"So," said Matt, "it really doesn't change the situation, or not until we know differently, and that's not likely to happen. The Cheyenne sent scouts to look over this wagon train, likely to see who it was and if they were going to cut them off from Cutter's Gap. The scouts got shot at. The Cheyenne retaliated, which is not surprising, knowing the Cheyenne. No man worth his salt would have done differently. So we're still on a round-'em-up-and-herd-'em-home mission. And we'd better do it fast, before word of this massacre leaks out. A lot of folks will likely be a hell of a lot less understanding, including our own regimental HQ."

Allison, Chubb, and Olsen understood and agreed.

"Mr. Fox, did you find out anything?" Matt asked.

"Not really," Fox replied. "A number of these folks were killed in their beds, so to speak, and it sort of looks like there was some kind of sickness going around, but that's not too unusual among parties of pilgrims like these. It does kind of explain why they didn't put up more of a fight, though. Could've been anything—bad water, food poisoning, who knows? *They're* not telling, that's for sure."

Of course, had a real doctor been present, the dead would have told him a great deal, and would have provided Easy Company with a warning concerning these Indians' exposure to a disease against which they had no resistance whatever. . . .

But as it was, Fox's report gave no cause for alarm, and there was still the pressing matter of getting the Indians back to the reservation before any further tragedies occurred.

"Right, then," said Matt, since there seemed to be nothing more to discuss. "Mr. Allison, you and Chubb take off after them. Try to catch them and turn them back. Maybe Smaldoon's gotten up the far side and has turned them already."

"Not with the runs, he hasn't," said Allison.

"Oh, yeah, that's right," said Matt, having heard about Smaldoon's problem. "Anyway, stay on their tail and try to turn them. Smaldoon'll be along sooner or later, even if Breckenridge has to carry him. I'll take care of the burials here and head back home. You keep us posted. If Smaldoon's not recovered, I'll head back up here myself. Is all that clear?"

Allison inclined his head a bit and gave Matt a brief salute. Chubb did the same.

Wearily, Matt returned the salutes, then set about his business as Allison led his men off toward Cutter's Gap.

eleven

Back at Easy Company, Amos Fletcher thought it was an especially good day. Not because the payroll had arrived, nor because he'd gotten word it was on the way. Rather, it was because the headaches, the pains in his bones and joints, the sore throat, the mild rash over his body, all had begun to lessen.

Yes, it was a good day. The rest of his gang, men and women, might still be suffering all those things he'd had, but he was healing. And it probably meant they'd heal up too, after a while.

What had happened, of course, was that the syphilis was beginning to pass from its secondary phase into a latent third phase, during which, hidden, it continued to destroy, kill, or cripple, that outcome occurring at any time during the latent period, depending on what part of the body—brain, heart, nervous system—was most severely affected.

Soon, no one would be able to guess what was killing Fletcher and thereby be able to treat it.

The only good aspect of the transition was that, once into the latent phase, the disease became considerably less contagious, if contagious at all. Pregnant women with latent syphilis could pass it along, or deliver flawed babies, but aside from that, the disease was a threat to none but the infected.

However, the rest of Fletcher's gang had not yet reached that relatively benign stage, and were active threats to everyone.

The women were especially active threats, an unnaturally sexual group as a whole, and less than satisfied by encounters within their gang alone. They were constantly on the prowl for randy soldiers.

If the soldiers only wouldn't keep getting sent off to fight Indians. . . .

Cassie Smaldoon was off on another errand, and her "unconscious" patient was on his feet again, prowling around the room, his strength returning rapidly. He now allowed himself to be fed in his unconscious state. Cassie thought that was remarkable, that he could eat while unconscious, and said as much to Maggie, whereupon Maggie repressed a smile. Actually, she not only repressed it, but instead looked and sounded very serious as she said, "Cassandra, that *is* remarkable. It may not be ladylike for me to mention this, but . . . while we've been washing him and changing his bandages . . . have you noticed the size of his genitals?"

While Cassie had gasped and her eyes had popped, Maggie had noticed the "unconscious" man start slightly, then twitch, his eyeballs rolling around beneath his eyelids. "Well," said Maggie, "it's lucky he's unconscious and can't hear me. Dear me, aren't I awful?"

Now, as he prowled back and forth, the patient remembered the occasion and smiled. Maggie was onto him, that was for sure. But he was glad she hadn't let on to Cassie. Once Cassie knew he was conscious, he was going to have to talk himself blue in the face, telling her all about himself, and though she was a very attractive woman, he wasn't ready for that. Not yet.

He passed the window again, carefully, and glanced out. And froze.

Amos Fletcher had wandered in from the camp just outside the walls and was standing in front of the sutler's store, basking in the sun and celebrating his returning health.

The man in Smaldoon's quarters stood as still as ice and stared at Fletcher. That face was familiar, even at that distance, through pictures and descriptions. That man was Amos Fletcher.

He didn't know how long he'd stood there staring out the window, scarcely breathing, but suddenly there was a cool voice behind him, asking crisply, "I don't suppose you happen to know where Cassie's gone?"

His head swiveled slowly and he stared at Maggie Cohen, the intent expression still on his face. It almost frightened Maggie. But then his face softened. And then, his voice touched with amusement, he said, "No, I don't know where she is, Maggie. But as long as she's gone, I should take the opportunity to inform you that my genitals are of only average proportions. Which should tell you something about the person you're comparing me to."

"I didn't mean that," said Maggie. "I only wanted to see if you were playing possum." She scowled and added, "You ain't no bigger than Ben, so there."

"You won't tell Cassie?"

"That you're only average?" she teased.

"No. That I'm conscious. Just for a while?"

Maggie nodded.

"Now tell me, who's that man?" And his face went icy again as he turned to look back out the window.

As they looked out at Fletcher, the main gate swung open and the Sanitary Corps wagons, bearing the dead and wounded from the agency fight, slowly rolled in.

Lance Corporal Enright reported to Sergeant Cohen, "Corps here with the wounded, Sarge. Where'll we put them?"

"Enlisted day room. And then tell the ladies they've got some work, 'ceptin' Cassie, who's already got a patient, and Flora—Maggie'll tell Flora."

Enright carried out the instructions. Soon, about half a dozen Sanitary Corps soldiers, a few missionaries, and one of Agent Mallory's men were spread out all over the day room, on cots, being tended by the women of the post, who were never displeased to be pressed into this type of service.

"Two died on the way," said Lieutenant Marlowe to Captain Conway, on the parade outside the day room. "We packed them in with the rest of the dead." He nodded his head toward one of the wagons.

There was a shriek from inside the day room. Both men started, but then Marlowe smiled. "We also picked up one living on the way. The fellow that got shot down riding with Miss Selby. She must have just discovered him. Anyway, you'd

better get *them*"—he gestured toward the wagon of dead men—
"into the ground fast."

Captain Conway snapped some orders, and Corporal Bab-
cock, squad leader of Second Platoon's only remaining squad,
the First, led several privates out the gate, double-timing with
spades at port arms.

A hole was dug some twenty yards from the post walls, in
an area already spotted with grave markers, and the hearse
wagon was then drawn outside and the bodies buried.

The Reverend McElroy spoke a few words over the mass
gravesite, his voice for once lowered, reverent, and movingly
solemn.

Amos Fletcher and his gang watched all of it with their eyes
blinking furiously. There seemed to be a hell of a lot going on
for a post that was damn near empty. It also seemed to be
filling up again pretty fast.

It didn't help their peace of mind that the burial ground was
about ten yards from where their camp was pitched. They
thought about moving the camp. Bad luck, camping in a graveyard. Everybody knew that.

"How come you didn't know it was a graveyard?" asked
Amos of the man who'd set up camp.

"I knowed it," said the man. "Jes' didn't bother me none.
Figgered it'd be peaceful."

"Peaceful! Whole troop o' sojers diggin' in yer front yard.
Preacher blessin' our camp 'long with the grave." Amos suddenly started giggling.

"Lucky we didn't have to do the diggin'," said Jeff Dow to
Private John "Weasel" Gillies, a little fellow from the New
York slums to whom the army had given self-respect and a
future.

"How come?" responded Gillies, who was not fond of Dow.
"*I* don't mind diggin'."

"That's 'cause you can't dig much," Dow shot back. "That's
why. I'd have to dig *for* you."

"I can outdig you any day of the damn week," said Gillies,
who, at about fourteen years of age, had worked a stretch as
a sandhog.

Dow shrugged. "Don't matter. Diggin' ain't my specialty.
Fightin' is." He eyed Gillies. He'd heard that Weasel was a
nasty opponent, despite his size. "Pisses the hell outa me, bein'
left off all these patrols. If there's anything I admire, it's gettin'

an Injun squared up in my sights. Poweee! One more dead Injun."

Weasel regarded Dow silently, thinking that there were some people who should never have a gun put in their hands; this asshole was obviously one of them.

Sergeant Cohen marched across the parade, flanked by Mess Sergeant Dutch Rothausen and Supply Sergeant Skinflint Wilson. "With all my NCOs gone," said Ben, "you two may have to double up on some of the duties."

Both sergeants looked exceedingly unhappy. "I got doctorin' *besides* cookin'," claimed Rothausen.

"Doc Marlowe's back," Cohen reminded him. "And Anson can handle Supply for a while," he told Sergeant Wilson, referring to the supply clerk, Corporal Anson Clark, a mysterious creature who rarely emerged from the supply room, even to the extent of sleeping there, a shotgun by his bunk, as a result of which habit there was damned little supply thievery at Easy.

The three sergeants came upon a group of privates that included Gillies and Dow.

"Well," Cohen said, "if ever I seen a bunch of men who was born to dig a latrine.... You're in charge, Dutch. All right, boys, Sergeant Rothausen here will show you how diggin's done at Penn State."

"Sergeant Cohen," Dow wheedled, "I know I oughta hang around an' help with the diggin', but—"

"We're short, Dow."

"I know, Sarge, but I gotta make up my mind real quick about re-upping, which means me and the widder got a lot to talk about yet...."

Cohen was beginning to wonder whether he really wanted Dow to reenlist, the man was getting to be such a pain in the ass. "All right, Dow," he finally said. "Take off. But you got just another week, then you gotta shit or get off the pot."

"He'll prob'ly do both at the same time," said Weasel. "Dow usually *talks* about diggin' more'n he *digs*."

"Okay, boys," said Dutch authoritatively, "let's start diggin'."

"Where, Sarge? And with what?"

Dutch turned to Sergeant Cohen. "How long's this gonna go on, Ben?"

"Matt's on his way back now, Dutch. Which means Gus'll be along pretty soon."

"Not soon enough," grumbled Dutch. "And you're guessin' about Kincaid." He took a deep breath. "Okay," he yelled, "you boys know where the goddamn shovels are. Go get 'em!"

Jeff Dow was striding toward the barracks to pick up some equipment when a large man fell in beside him—Jack Diamond, a shaggy man, slow and methodical but precise. And huge. Diamond had just gotten off guard, a later shift than Dow's. He'd seen Dow slip free of the latrine detail, and he surmised the reason—Dow's affairs were no big secret in the barracks, mainly due to Dow's own big mouth. "You heading over to the widow's place?" he asked.

Dow looked up at him sourly. "Yeah. What's it to you?" He didn't like Diamond, but had always found him easy to push around; Diamond, like many really big men, was especially careful about using his natural power. It made him a patsy for the likes of Dow.

"Thought maybe I could tag along."

"Ain't you got nothin' to do? They're kinda short here just now, y'know."

"You're *supposed* to have the day free, after getting off guard. But if I hang around, I know they'll find something for me to do. I saw them almost get you just now."

Dow thought about it. The widow was sure to have some unpleasant task awaiting him. It was as if she were testing him. Well, this time she had a surprise in store. Jeff was going to have a little helper along. He grinned. "Sure. Why not? You can drool over what I got waitin' for me."

Cassie Smaldoon and Maggie Cohen were walking along under the overhang that ran around the entire inside perimeter of the post. They'd walked from the officers' and dependents' mess, past the orderly room, and were just coming up on Smaldoon's quarters. "I was just talking to Lieutenant Marlowe," said Cassie. "I asked him if it was unusual for a man to stay unconscious this long, especially when it didn't seem like he had a head injury."

"And?"

"He said it was, said he'd drop by and take a look."

"Ah," said Maggie. "Let me talk to him and arrange it. I'd like to be there when he shows up."

Cassie opened the door to the Smaldoon quarters and they walked in.

The first thing they noticed was that the bed was empty. Cassie's heart leaped up to her throat.

The second thing they saw was the bounty man, standing with his back to them, staring at himself in a full-length mirror. And he was something to stare at. He was wearing Cassie's nightgown—they had been alternating it with Fox's pajamas—and as he stood there, it looked especially ridiculous, stretched to the breaking point across his broad shoulders and reaching down only as far as his knees. But what made it appear even more outrageous was the gunbelt that he had strapped around his hips.

At the moment he was checking one of his Colts, twirling the chamber. He saw the women and turned slowly, dropping the Colt into the right-hand holster.

He did not cross-draw from belt height, as did the army. Rather, his heavily laden holsters hung flat against the sides of his hips, several inches below the waist, the classic gun-fighter's positioning.

"Miss Cassie," he said to the astonished girl, and "Mrs. Cohen," to the narrow-eyed Maggie. "Wasn't expecting you back so quick."

"Evidently," said Maggie. "D'you think you're strong enough to handle those things?"

Maggie found herself suddenly staring down the barrel of the right-hand Colt. She'd barely seen him move. The left one, though, was a little slower clearing. "Not yet," he said, "but I'm getting there. Damage seems to be healing up on the left side a mite slower than the right."

Cassie finally found her voice. "You've been *conscious* all this time? Playing possum?"

"Some," he admitted.

"While . . . while . . . while your bandages were being changed?"

"Can't say as I remember *that*," he lied. "Seein' the fine ladies you are, though, and considerin' the extent of the damage, I 'spect you spared yourself the ugliness and embarrassment and had one or two of the men take care of them functions. Leastways, I hope you did. It'd be awful mortifyin' to me to think different."

"Oh, no, *no*, you're right," said Cassie. "We had Dutch take care of it. He's the mess sergeant."

"A *cook*?"

"And there's a doctor here too. The one that sewed you up."

"Ah. *Him* I'd like to meet."

"And who, sir," asked Maggie with leaden politeness, "shall we say wants to meet him?"

He seemed to ponder this for a moment. Finally he said, "I owe you. And I owe the doctor. But I don't want my name getting to anyone else, do you understand me?"

"Oh, my God," said Cassie. "You're an *outlaw.*"

"No," he said evenly, "I'm not. But I must have your word. For your own good and for the safety of others."

"You have it," said Maggie.

"John," he said. "John Pickett."

Maggie's eyes became slits, but Cassie squawked, "Who's Rachel? And those other names?"

"Rachel?" A look of deep sorrow came into his eyes. "My sister. And I don't know what other names I mentioned, but they were probably her children."

"Ah," said Cassie, relieved.

Pickett understood. She was living in a different world from the one he now occupied. He wondered if he would ever again cross back over to her world.

twelve

Dow and Diamond rode slowly toward the widow Bennett's spread. It was a fine summer day. A handful of clouds, big, lumpy blobs of cotton, scudded across the blue sky, their shadows racing over the prairie below them.

"Ever think you might go so fast you'd lose your shadow?" asked Diamond of Jeff Dow.

Dow stared at him. What a stupid question.

"Injuns figure that if you lose your shadow," said Diamond, unperturbed, "you're as good as dead."

"Ain't that the truth? Ain't no shadows six feet under."

"That's not what they mean. Besides, Injuns don't bury their dead. They stick 'em up on platforms."

"Buzzards get 'em."

"They're supposed to, or else they just rot away until only the bones are left. Then they likely take the bones and hide 'em away somewheres."

"You mean like in them sacred burial grounds? I thought they buried the whole damn body."

Diamond didn't know what sacred grounds Dow was thinking of, and didn't care. Getting a decent conversation out of him was like digging for worms in a dungheap. This widow had to be either desperate or not all that Dow claimed she was.

"How much longer you got, Diamond? I got about a week."

Jack Diamond sighed. "About two months."

"That's all? How come you ain't said nothin'? Ah, I getcha. You're gonna re-up anyways, so what's the point?"

Diamond nodded slowly, but he wasn't sure. He only knew he wasn't going back East, back to New London, back to whaling.

He'd lost his father and brothers to whaling. Then he'd gone out himself and it had scared him shitless. He didn't like the water, not deep water anyway, not *oceans*. So he hadn't lasted long.

It had both disappointed and pleased his mother, finding she had a son who would not die at sea. It shamed his sisters and puzzled his friends. So he'd left New London.

He'd gone into the army for the tail end of the War. Then he'd farmed for a while, and was good at it, but it was a lonely life and he had trouble meeting women; he was big and awkward and no beauty.

That had been ten years earlier. He'd drifted for a while, then gone back into the army. And after three years, he'd reenlisted for three more, but only because there wasn't anything else he'd wanted to do.

They'd sent him West in 1874. He was not a great soldier, but many who were had gotten themselves killed.

He liked the Plains. There wasn't an ocean within a thousand miles in any direction.

"Ever sail a ship?" he asked.

"Sure. Used to raft down the Ohio," Dow replied.

"It ain't the same," said Diamond.

"Sure it is. Water's water."

"No it ain't."

They finally drew rein in front of the widow's sod home. Diamond eyed it critically. Despite his distaste for the whaling life, he measured everything against the solidity with which whaling ships were built. Outpost Number Nine came close to meeting his standards, but whatever the late Bennett's talents, building had not been one of them.

The widow Bennett emerged, a wide smile stiff on her face.

"Jeffrey. What a pleasure—I didn't expect you. And you've brought a friend."

Dow's face clouded. He said curtly, "This is Diamond."

Diamond wondered silently how Dow had stumbled on this. The widow Bennett was beautiful, he thought—mature, full-bodied, nice dark hair. He was certain that any man would find her at least pretty. Nice looking, anyway. A bit worn around the edges maybe, but hell, life on the High Plains was no picnic.

He wondered what her appeal to Dow was. Dow wasn't bad looking and said he was a ladies' man. Was it the property that made the widow appealing to him? It was puzzling. A spread like this needed work, and Dow was a lazy bastard.

Hell, the widow was about to make herself a bad deal. But it wasn't any of Diamond's business.

"Isn't your friend going to light and stay awhile?" the widow asked.

Just then, Naomi came out. Diamond blinked, startled at the sight of the widow's luscious daughter. He alighted quickly from his mount, yanking off his hat in the same motion. His size, as he stood on the ground, plainly awed the two women.

"Pleased to make your acquaintance, ma'am," he told Mrs. Bennett. "And Miss . . ."

"Naomi," the girl said, smiling.

"Naomi," he echoed, returning the smile.

"Well, now that I'm here," Dow broke in, "what've you got for me to do? The chicken coop? You been savin' the chickenshit for me?"

"Jeffrey!" the widow blurted, blushing.

"Aw, ol' Diamond don't mind," Dow said. "He's a sojer."

But Diamond did mind. He didn't hold with that kind of loose talk around womenfolk.

"Chickenshit's chickenshit, Ma," said Naomi. "Ain't no other way to call it."

Oh, well, Diamond thought. Young'uns likely grew up harder out here on the frontier.

"Well, what're you waitin' for, Jack?" Dow said. "Shovel's in the barn. I'll be along in two shakes." He took the older woman by the arm and hustled her off toward the house.

Diamond turned and walked thoughtfully toward the barn. Naomi watched his massive, retreating back for a moment, then turned and walked toward the house herself.

Her mother was heating a pot of coffee and Dow was sitting at the kitchen table when she came in. He turned a lecherous smile on her and said, "C'mere, gal, give yer *per*-spective pa a hug."

She did so, and they clung together as long as the widow stared down at her pot. Finally the widow turned, resurrected the broad smile and they parted.

"Well, then," said the widow, "is it all set?"

"Set as can be. Just a few more days and then it's . . . together unto *ee*-ternity."

The widow wasn't sure she liked the sound of that. Sounded like a suicide pact. "That'll be nice."

"Hell, you don't sound too happy 'bout it."

Naomi scowled while her mother said, "It's just been a hard day. You certainly spoke roughly to your friend. Do you talk like that to all your friends?"

"Sure. If they wanna be my friends, they take it. As for Diamond, he ain't really no friend. He just ast if he could come along, get away from the post."

"Maybe he'd like some coffee."

"Naw, he don't need no coffee. Let 'im work."

Mrs. Bennett didn't like that. There were a lot of things she didn't like about Dow, but what was she to do? Between Naomi and the spread, she hadn't had time to meet much of anyone, and those she'd met hadn't impressed her, until Jeff Dow had swept down into their yard to ask for water. Cut a real fine figure. And she'd been flattered by his attention. Arnold Bennett had been twenty years her senior and a sour old prune.

"Are you sure we're doing the right thing, Jeff?" she asked.

"*I'm* sure. Why, I'm willing to give up my freedom for you and little Naomi here. But you gotta decide for yourself, Zelly." Dow felt like a man holding a straight flush. "Tell you what—lemme give you a little more persuadin'."

Giselle Bennett frowned.

"Naomi," Dow continued, "whyn't you take a walk and see how ol' Diamond's doin'? And don't come back for a while."

Naomi smiled secretively.

"Now you go on," said Dow, smiling right back, insinuating all the mystery he could manage, "git yourself along. Me and your ma, we got things to . . . talk about."

Naomi fought back a grin, biting her lip. Then she left. But she didn't go far, just around to a side door, where a crack between the door and its frame provided a place where she knew she could hear anything that was said in the kitchen.

". . . Now you and me, Zelly, let's take ourselves off to that bed of yours. I think you need some convincin'."

"The coffee, Jeff . . ."

"To hell with it. I don't need that. You know what I need. All you can talk about is coffee, while I'm talkin' about *love*."

"No you're not," she said very quietly.

"What's that? I didn't hear," Dow said.

"I said I think it may be that time of month."

His face fell. "You mean you're bleedin'?"

She nodded.

"Again? You were jes' bleedin' a few weeks ago."

"It's the curse of being a woman, Jeff."

Dow took a deep breath.

"I can feel it coming, I can always feel it coming."

"You mean it ain't *here* yet? Then c'mon, we'll—"

"No, Jeff, not now."

Dow flared up. "No? Not now? Well, ain't that a fine how-de-do. Make a man feel real wanted."

"Jeff," said the widow softly, "why don't I just fix some coffee, and we can talk and . . . and snuggle . . . and maybe you can help that man. . . ."

Jeff Dow could barely restrain his irritation. "Oh, hell, I jes' remembered, I tol' the captain I was headed this way, and"—he looked stricken—"and he kinda talked me into sayin' I'd pick up some toilet water for him in town. For him and the missus. Wait'll you meet 'em, you'll like 'em. I'm gonna invite 'em to the weddin'. But I better get goin' if I'm gonna get that stuff. Damn! Tell Jack I'll be back in a bit, all right?" He yelled that last bit as he was going out the door. He almost ran into Naomi, but didn't even see her as he leaped on his horse and rode out.

Naomi ran into the house, into the kitchen. "You were *mean* to him!" she cried. "He's gonna go away and never come back!"

"He'll be back," said Giselle Bennett wearily, not daring to wonder why the thought brought no joy. "He had an important errand to run in town."

Naomi turned and ran from the house, running over the fields toward the scarecrow.

Sadly, Giselle watched her run. Naomi needed someone, needed a father. All she had was a scarecrow. That had been a terrible idea, dressing those sticks of wood up in Arnold's good suit.

The widow wandered toward the chicken house, wondering why there was no sign of activity.

She reached the chicken house and peered inside. It was empty—but also, amazingly, clean. Jeff usually spent an entire day cleaning it out. Then she heard the sound of hammering. She followed the sound around to the rear, northern side of the barn.

There she found Jack Diamond at work, practically rebuilding the entire wall.

His mouth was full of nails, so he couldn't speak for a while, but when he could, he asked, "When was the last time you had anyone around what knew what he was doing? Or did you ever?" He didn't seem to care who he insulted.

"Arnold was good with his hands," she said defensively.

"Not so you'd notice," he replied. Who the hell was Arnold? he thought.

The widow studied what Diamond had done so far. She'd learned to know good work, and had concluded privately that Arnold had not been especially expert. And this, what Diamond was doing, was good work.

"And Jeff?" she said, giving him her first true smile of the day.

Diamond, scowling at a nail, said, "Jeff's handy with his *mouth*."

Jeff Dow paused long enough in town to buy a small bottle of toilet water, and then he headed for Annie's Saloon.

Annie wasn't much, a grizzled old hag, but she was a pretty fair madam and she had Jeff fixed up in no time with Rosie, Pride of the Plains.

Pride of the dogs, thought Dow, but taste had never been a strong point with him. Appetite and satisfaction, those were his strengths, and he wondered if the widow wasn't going to fall short. She was always having the goddamn curse.

But it *was* security. A man had to think about that. Hell, what was Cohen talkin' about, if it wasn't security—three squares and a bed and get paid for it besides, he'd say.

It was about three hours later that Dow rode back into the Bennett yard. Naomi sat by the front door. She looked at him and then glared toward the barn.

Jeff saw Diamond and the widow emerge from the barn. Giselle was talking animatedly to Diamond, who was listening attentively but stoically.

Giselle looked up and saw Dow, and though he couldn't see it from where he was, she blushed. She ran to him and practically pulled him from the saddle.

"Jeff! Your friend has done such marvelous work! And he was just showing me what else there is to do. So *much*.... But right now, you come on inside. Naomi, will you show Mr. Diamond the fields, show him what's been planted? *Naomi*? You go ahead and do what I ask, you hear?"

Naomi stood up and slouched toward Diamond, who observed her approach with equal enthusiasm.

Meanwhile, the widow had hauled Jeff Dow into the house, right past the kitchen and into her bedroom. "I hope your captain appreciates what you did," she said, "depriving me of your company all day."

Jeff Dow wondered what the hell she had in mind.

She began to undo her dress, feigned difficulty, and turned around, saying, "Undo me, Jeff."

"Ain't you got the curse?" he asked distastefully.

"I was mistaken, Jeff, and a man like you, a healthy man, well, I know he needs a woman, needs her often."

"Well, now, Zelly," he said, not touching the laces, "I done give it a lot of thought. Ridin' all that way ... I done some thinkin'.... We're so close to gettin' hitched, maybe we better not give little Naomi the wrong impression. Maybe we oughta wait until we're really hitched, then I'll carry you across the threshold and we'll do it right. How's that sound?"

"Do you really mean it, Jeff? You're not just not going to bed with me ... just to please me, are you? Because I'm willing—"

"Yes 'n' no, Zelly, yes 'n' no. Pleasin' you is about all I wanna do, all that means anything to me...."

"Well, maybe we will wait, then. Maybe...." She was going to have to rethink all her previous impressions of Jeff Dow. The man had more nobility in him than she'd suspected.

They came back out of the house, smiling and arm in arm. Diamond and Naomi, trudging unhappily, hadn't gone very far.

Naomi ran back and flung herself into Jeff's arms while Giselle Bennett beamed approvingly.

110

Diamond watched Jeff's hands, the eagerness with which he grasped the young girl, and he scowled and went to untie his horse.

thirteen ═══════════════

Hungry Buffalo led his village through Cutter's Gap. He himself rode in the center of the procession, which, due to the narrowness of the gap, was strung out for some distance. With him were the elders, the women and children, and the heavily laden, pony-drawn travois. Half of the warriors rode at the head, half at the rear.

Hungry Buffalo, who'd recently risen to the position of chief through seniority and non-association with the previous year's string of defeats, was the best possible leader at that time. Though ready to fight at any moment, like any Cheyenne, he'd already experienced enough war to bring sense to the present situation. He knew that theirs was not a war expedition, as the young hotheads chose to believe, but rather a flight to freedom and safety—to the mountains. And he knew that beyond this cleft in the ridge lay a vast plain that had to be crossed before the mountain haven would be theirs. The blue-clad Americans, whom they'd eluded back at the reservation, would surely be chasing them.

Encountering the wagon train, and having to attack it, had been unfortunate. It had filled the young warriors with blood-lust, and filled the village with happiness. Hungry Buffalo had yelled himself hoarse limiting his warriors to the mere taking of scalps, preventing the time-consuming mutilation in which the Cheyenne sometimes indulged. He'd also had to prevent any scalp-dancing, which might have proved a critical waste of precious hours.

Hungry Buffalo had had to restate the purpose of their flight, pointing out the vulnerability of their women and children and the difference in fighting temper and ability between the wagon train's feeble Americans and the Blue Sleeves. The Blue Sleeves liked to fight as much as the Cheyenne did, and fought just as hard and well. Many of the youngest warriors did not know that, or believe it, but Hungry Buffalo assured them it was true.

And so he pushed his people on through the gap, hoping for a clear path ahead and crippled horses for their pursuit. If his medicine was strong, it would be so.

Crying Eagle rode at the head of the column, White Bull by his side. Neither of them had believed Hungry Buffalo. The Americans had fought well at the reservation, but only from desperation. The Americans with the wagon train had hardly fought at all, many just lying there waiting to be killed. No, the Americans were not enemies to be greatly feared, especially not when the Cheyenne outnumbered them, and certainly not in hand-to-hand combat, when coups were to be counted.

Hungry Buffalo had instructed them to watch for the Americans and seek to avoid them. They watched for the Americans, all right, but to attack. They would remind Hungry Buffalo, wise though he was, what young blood could accomplish.

Unfortunately, no Americans were in sight when at length they led the column from the gap, but only a vast, rolling sea of grass that extended to distant, hazy blue mountains.

Crying Eagle sighed. "The Americans will come from behind. The Bowstring Soldiers and the Elk Horn Scrapers will get to count coups." Crying Eagle belonged to the Kit Fox Society, and they, along with the Dog Soldiers, led the procession.

"Only if the attack comes soon," said White Bull. "The village will be through before the shadows lengthen, and then we will be joined and share the coups."

Crying Eagle nodded. "The Blue Sleeves will linger where we killed the Americans. They are soft and will waste much precious time."

With every hurried step, their chances for battle seemed to diminish. How was a man to gain honor if not through battle? Hungry Buffalo's strategy was clearly self-serving. But they did have the village to think about. "If it were not for the women and children, we could turn back and go find the Americans."

But instead they continued to press ahead. And soon the village was through the gap and had drawn into a more compact group with a tight center, ringed by warriors. The whole then moved on rapidly, tired but responding to the urgings of Hungry Buffalo. But it wasn't long before their dreams—or Hungry Buffalo's dreams—collapsed, and the hearts of Crying Eagle and the warriors leaped.

They'd followed a slight depression onto an open, flat stretch and were well onto it when they saw, to the west, rising up along the top of a far, sharp rise, a long string of mounted men. Soldiers.

Lieutenant Smaldoon had pushed his men through the night at a fierce pace, faster than either Kincaid or Allison had dared. Peter, the scout, found himself moving much faster than he would have liked, or thought safe, as the platoon kept threatening to run up his heels, if not actually pass him.

When dawn broke they were still riding hard, and Peter was happy to see the ridge running north off to his right, to the east. He'd been pushed so hard he'd lost his bearings during the night, but hadn't wanted to admit it.

"Scout's good," said Smaldoon. "Brought us dead on."

Breckenridge smiled. Sixty miles back, the scout had angled to the right and Breckenridge had taken the column to the left. It had taken Peter fifteen minutes to catch up. Now Peter glanced back at Breckenridge with a look of gratitude. The sergeant stared back impassively. He'd taken a patrol up that way not three weeks previously. He simply knew the way.

Peter now kicked his horse to a faster gait. He rode light, without a saddle, and he was slight himself, and the horse had enough strength left to move away from the column.

"Think maybe we better slow down?" asked Smaldoon. Now that it was light, he'd noticed the condition of the horses, and with battle in mind, it worried him.

"How's Cassie doing with that patient of hers?" responded Breckenridge, subtly asking his mount for a little bit more speed.

"How the hell would I know?" yelled Smaldoon, successfully distracted. "I don't live there."

"Thought you did."

"I live with Mr. Maynard Fox. Buttercup."

Breckenridge turned the name Buttercup over in his mind, smiling. "You ever see that big dude that works in the blacksmith shop in town? Helps Riley out sometimes?"

"I don't know the names of the townspeople, but I know the man. Muscles. Doesn't talk, just makes noises."

"That's the feller. Well, he made some noises at Mr. Fox a few weeks back. Mr. Fox acted real polite but wanted some questions answered. Feller wouldn't, tried to push Mr. Fox clear. Ol' Buttercup invited him out back in a real nice way and beat the crap out of him. It was awful."

Smaldoon chewed that over for a while, and Breckenridge reflected on the number of times he'd had to cover some officer's backside.

"I wouldn't have thought he'd take kindly to being called Buttercup," said Breckenridge.

Probably wouldn't, decided Smaldoon. Fortunately he hadn't gotten around to calling Fox that to his face.

Just then his horse stumbled jarringly. "Sergeant," he said, "don't you think we ought to be going a little slower? The horses won't be fit for anything."

"They ain't gotta be, sir. We just gotta git there."

"What if we have to chase the hostiles?"

"Ain't s'posed to. Jes' cut 'em off. Leastways that was *my* understanding. Captain tell you somethin' different, sir?"

Smaldoon ground his teeth together and began to brood. Breckenridge admired the weather. He also let the horses slow a bit, but solely out of regard for the horses.

After a few hours of near-silence, Breckenridge said, "We got something."

Smaldoon saw Peter riding back toward them, his rifle raised high and pumping up and down.

They stopped. The horses' tongues lolled from the sides of their mouths. Peter rode up and pointed to the northeast.

"Two mile there, cross flat, go west. Maybe two hundred Cheyenne."

Hot damn, thought Smaldoon. Now, if he could only attack,

he might be able to start shining up some silver first lieutenant's bars. "Where are they headed?" he asked. "What's in
front of them?"

"Hill."

"Hill? A big one or a small one?"

"Middle."

Smaldoon tried to envision a middle-sized hill.

"Think I know it, sir," said Breckenridge. "It's a long rise.
But they'll go right over it; it ain't that steep."

"Can we beat them there?" asked Smaldoon.

"Ride like hell," said Peter.

Dammit, they'd *been* riding like hell. Smaldoon's backside
told him so, would have told him so even without it's being
softened up by the runs. Jesus, the misery he'd endured. Nobody *knew*.

"Well, sir?" wondered Breckenridge.

"Ride like hell and walk the last quarter-mile, likely. But
let's go."

So they rode, and finally rose up in a line atop the hill to
confront the advancing Cheyenne.

Smaldoon grated, "If those bastards dare to attack..." He
didn't think they would.

But Breckenridge said, "They might, sir. They've got some
loonies amongst 'em. We'd best discourage them."

They all gladly dismounted.

"Let's show them we mean business, Sergeant," said Smaldoon, which was exactly what Breckenridge had suggested.

"Corporal Kane," called Sergeant Breckenridge, "detail
someone to collect the horses and get 'em back outa sight.
Rafferty, Sprague, Mitchell, you three are going to do the
actual firing."

Crying Eagle and White Bull, along with the rest, continued
to eye the soldiers, now hunkered down on the far rise.

Hungry Buffalo rode up.

"There are only a few," said Crying Eagle, having made
an accurate count. "We can take them easily."

"Not easily," said Hungry Buffalo. "They have the high
ground."

"Yellow Hair did too, at the Greasy Grass," Crying Eagle
argued, "and Crazy Horse taught us how to circle and come
from the side." He eyed the empty ridge flanking the soldiers,
and his mouth watered.

"And taught the Americans to watch out for those tactics," countered Hungry Buffalo. "And there may be more Americans, many more, hiding on the other side of the hill." He smiled a thin, intelligent smile. "Old Cheyenne trick."

The Cheyenne soldier societies, combined, had been known to overrule the chief, but not this time. Crying Eagle had to admit Hungry Buffalo was right.

Just then there were three puffs of smoke from the distant line of soldiers. The three slugs disappeared into the grass some fifty yards to the front of them, but they heard the rifle reports. "And they may have the long guns," Hungry Buffalo pointed out, referring to the Sharps, with its enormous range. He'd never known the army to use them, but he'd seen braves picked off by nervous hunters, several times. And the Indians sometimes took them from dead hunters and used them. "Let us go north," Hungry Buffalo continued. "They will have to move. We will then see their number, and be able to tell how hard they mean to press us." He wasn't discounting the possibility of having to fight clear; he just wanted to make sure it was necessary, and what kind of fight it would entail.

The village started moving again, but northward, paralleling the rise where the soldiers waited.

"Mount up!" cried Sergeant Breckenridge, and the order was met with a chorus of groans.

With dismay, Smaldoon watched the Cheyenne village moving away. "All we can do is follow them," he said disgustedly.

"That's about it, sir," Breckenridge agreed. "Just keep contact until Mr. Kincaid or Mr. Allison can head 'em off."

Smaldoon clawed his way back up onto his horse. "Damn thing's gotten taller," he muttered.

"Beggin' your pardon, sir," Breckenridge said, springing lightly up into his saddle, "but maybe if the lieutenant could show the men a little more grit . . ."

Smaldoon stared openmouthed at his platoon sergeant.

"Sit a little straighter, sir?" Breckenridge pressed mercilessly. "For the men, sir? 'Pears to me they're gettin' a mite depressed."

The Cheyenne kept an eye on the soldiers as they moved north. The sun beginning to dip toward the horizon, and the soldiers were truly casting long shadows.

They also sent scouts out to determine the actual size of

117

Smaldoon's force; the reports were encouraging.

"They are so few in number," mused Hungry Buffalo. 'If we cannot get around them...Crying Eagle, take your men and ride around them and attack along the ridge."

Crying Eagle did so. He led his men north a distance, then west along a draw, and then climbed up onto the ridge and charged down it, thirty braves riding hard, the late sun glinting off their weapons.

But where were the Americans? They were not atop the rise.

Slugs suddenly whistled overhead, followed by the crack of Springfields.

Smaldoon had pulled his men back off the rise, burying them in dense cover, from which they watched the Cheyenne "attack" and their subsequent confusion.

Crying Eagle knew where the shots were coming from, but couldn't see anyone. He turned his men around and rode back off the rise, heading back for the main body of the band. Only after a while did he realize that they'd been well within the range of the soldiers. Either the soldiers were very poor shots or they'd missed purposely.

Crying Eagle put his hand to his forehead.

It was warm and beaded with moisture. But the day was not hot. It might have been a sign of fear, but never before had he shown fear in battle.

The Cheyenne war party rejoined the village and explained what had happened. Hungry Buffalo, despite his wisdom, had no explanation.

They continued north.

Suddenly they were confronted by soldiers, a half-mile distant and beginning to take up positions.

The Cheyenne were amazed. The Americans had to have ridden like the wind to have gotten ahead of them.

But there they were, still atop that high rise, following them. Who, then, were these new Americans?

They were, of course, Mr. Allison, Sergeant Chubb, and elements of Third Platoon. Scout Robert Longtrees had scouted the action to their front and they'd skirted to the north to cut off that escape route.

The Cheyenne stopped. The enemy had suddenly doubled in number. Now the Americans would surely attack.

Hungry Buffalo drew his people together and prepared their defense. They would stay where they were, hold their ground.

The Americans would have to attack them, come out in the open. The Cheyenne would then cut them down, or let them come close and count many coups.

But as the sun slowly set, the attack did not come.

And night fell.

By morning, half of Hungry Buffalo's warriors were beginning to show signs of illness: fever, chills, heavy perspiration. The ones who carried out the raid on the McClellan wagon train were the first to show the symptoms. They tried to hide their weakness, but many noticed it and told Hungry Buffalo.

Hungry Buffalo worried. The sickness was surely a sign, an omen, but of what? Did it mean they should press forward, or did it mean that their venture was not blessed by the gods?

He saw that the American forces were still arrayed as they had been the night before, and gave no sign of moving, either to retreat or attack, which further confused Hungry Buffalo and his council.

The chief decided to retire to the privacy of his tipi, to seek guidance from his medicine.

At the same time he ordered that exploratory feints be made at the enemy, to test their mettle, to discover their purpose.

Late that morning a brutal thunderstorm suddenly struck from the northwest, drenching the village—most families had not had the time or energy to erect tipis—and bringing with it chilly winds. If ever there was a sign begging to have meaning read from it, or read into it, the storm was it. But Hungry Buffalo's desire to return to the former peace of the reservation warred with the notion that he had been entrusted with a sacred mission to lead his people away from the Americans, away from the Black Robes and Long Needles, to the mountains and freedom.

And so he sat cross-legged and indecisive in his tipi, and water ran into the hastily raised shelter. The robes he sat on grew soaked and cold and unpleasant.

He knew that the rest of his people fared worse, but rain and cold could do no damage. The Americans were what worried him, along with the failure of his medicine to bring guidance.

fourteen

The thunderstorm rode the wind into Outpost Number Nine, along with Matt Kincaid and First Platoon. They'd seen it coming and raced the last couple of miles. As they rode in the gate, the thunder of their horses' hooves was scarcely distinguishable from that of the approaching storm. It was a thrilling sight to those who'd rarely seen a charging platoon of horse infantry, namely those Sanitary Corps personnel and missionaries who weren't busy tending to the sick and wounded. And to Amos Fletcher and his bunch, although to them it was as much depressing as thrilling.

But most of all it was exciting for the Culloch kids, who rode hellbent right along with the troops, staying with the men as they rode for the stables.

They all hit the ground running as the first large drops were beginning to fall, and crowded inside. Which might have been a disaster except that they were a disciplined military group, or, more to the point, they were Sergeant Olsen's disciplined men. They packed the stable in solid but orderly fashion, with hardly any fuss.

They stripped their horses of gear and rubbed them down, the NCOs and officers among them. It wasn't usual for Mr. Fox to care for his mount—there was always someone handy—but he saw Matt doing it and figured he'd better.

The Cullochs took take of their horses too, although little Enos needed a hand, since he was only able to work his from the belly down. Matt stripped the gear from Enos' horse after stripping his own and, after having taken care of his own animal, stepped over to tend to the upper half of Enos' mount.

He found Eleanora standing beside him, helping. He noticed the swell of her shirt and realized for the first time that she wasn't as young as he'd thought. She smiled shyly up at him and he returned a crooked grin.

"Bet you're sore from the ride," he said.

"I'm a little sore all over, sir," she said, "but I think it's just that we haven't gotten over lying in the back of that wagon, with those bodies on top of us. Matthew and Enos aren't feeling too well, either."

Enos glared up at her, as if to deny her statement.

"He isn't used to talking to anyone," she said. "Only me. Say hello, Enos. Say 'Thank you, sir.'"

Matt smiled down at the little boy and said, "You're not in the army, son. You don't have to call me 'sir,' My name's Matt."

The boy blinked, then turned and looked at his brother.

Eleanora laughed. "*His* name is Matt too. Matthew, actually. Are you—"

"Yep. But no one calls me that."

"I'm Malone."

"I'm Stretch."

"I'm—"

Kincaid turned to find himself and the girl surrounded by a group of grinning soldiers.

"All right, break it up," said Sergeant Olsen, pushing in among them. "You men finished your horses? Well, see that they're grained and then we'll wait for 'em to eat and cool down 'fore turnin' them loose. Maybe the rain'll have let up by then. I don't relish havin' to run the whole length of the goddamn parade in a goddamn downpour."

"Sergeant," said Malone, "would you please be mindin' your tongue, seein' how there's a lady present?"

Olsen almost went cross-eyed with embarrassment. Matt had to smile; Malone had nailed him fair and square. A fine,

121

if troublesome, sense of humor had Malone. It might mean trouble for Malone, though, unless Olsen forgot, which Olsen often did with unimportant things like this.

Malone turned away, trying to keep from laughing, and buried himself in the crowd. Matt distracted Olsen by saying, "Sergeant, see that everything's square here before you turn 'em loose."

This was unnecessary advice, and Olsen gave Matt a look that could kill.

"In the meantime," Matt went on, "I'm going to find these kids someplace to stay."

He led Eleanora, Matthew, and Enos away. Mr. Fox left too, seeing no reason *he* should hang around.

Matt, at Maggie's insistence, saw the three youngsters bunked in with the Cohens, which was an unsuspected break, since both Maggie and Ben had had measles as children and were therefore immune.

All three youngsters were beginning to complain of mild miseries, though Enos did so through his sister.

"You've been through a lot," said Matt. "Why don't you all just rest awhile."

"Good idea," said Maggie. "And I'll have some food brought over. You must be starving."

Eleanora and Matthew said they were. Enos whispered in Eleanora's ear. "Well, tell them, Enos," she said. "Go ahead, tell them. Don't be scared, they're nice people. He gave you a horseback ride, didn't he?"

Enos stared at Matt, at Maggie, then at a point in space between them. Finally he burst out, "I gotta go."

Matt smiled, took him by the hand, and led him outside and through the rain to the latrine. Enos' grip on Matt's hand grew tighter as they went.

Matt showed him inside, then said through the closed door, "Now you head on back to your sister when you're through, you hear?"

Silence.

"Did you hear me, Enos? Tell me if you did."

A muffled "Yes" came through the door. Matt smiled and walked off, heading for the day room. He was wet already, and didn't mind getting a bit wetter.

As he neared the day room, the door opened and Lieutenant Marlowe emerged. Marlowe looked wan; he'd been putting in long hours. But he brightened upon seeing Matt.

"Matt. Good to see you."

"Hi, Doc. How're the patients?"

"Lost some on the way back. Rest will make it, though. Including my latest miracle." He told of Forrest's amazing survival. "Just adds another to my list. Remember that man I patched, damn near had his innards blown away? He's up and about, damn near recovered. Man must have the constitution of a grizzly."

"Recovered?"

"Well, not really, of course. Lots still to heal up inside. But the muscle damage to the back wasn't extensive, and when it comes to moving around, that's important. Left side hasn't come back as quick as the right, but I hear tell he's moving quick, getting his strength back."

"Hear? You haven't seen him?"

"Well, no. I've been busy. But Cassie's let me know. Almost hourly. She thinks it's the miracle of Outpost Nine."

"What do you think?"

Doc Marlowe grinned. "Hell, I do too. I said so."

"Let's go take a look for ourselves."

John Pickett was sitting on his bed, legs dangling over the side, when Matt and Lieutenant Marlowe entered.

Pickett looked Matt over first, steadily, reading him as a man it didn't pay to mess with. Finally his gaze shifted to Marlowe and his look softened.

"Thank you, doctor," he said. When Marlowe looked puzzled he explained, "Cassie pointed you out."

"How do you feel?" Marlowe asked.

"Fine. Left side's a mite slow comin' back, but otherwise fine."

"Don't be too confident. As I was telling Matt, the muscles, especially the back muscles, escaped the most damage. But inside, it's going to take a while yet, a good while."

"Mmmm. I'm still not eating solid, but I'm in no hurry to go anywhere."

"Where *were* you going?" asked Matt.

"Here . . . there . . ." He shrugged.

"With a sackful of wanted circulars?"

"Never bothered to throw them away."

"Including the one for Cullen? Ray Cullen?"

What did Matt have in mind, Pickett wondered. "What about Cullen?"

"Well," said Matt, "I can understand your having Maxton's and Black Jack Berry's, they were nailed just about a month ago, down around Albuquerque. Our clerk keeps up on these things." Matt smiled. "But Cullen was shot and killed a year ago, down around Waco. How often do you clean out your saddlebags?"

"Not very often," he said. He hadn't known about Maxton and Berry, but Cullen had been a mistake, a finesse job by some joker who'd blown a man's face away and claimed it was Cullen. The man who'd done it had a manhunting rep and some manufactured evidence, and so was believed. But Cullen had never been anywhere near Waco, in fact no closer than he was at that very moment, sitting under the overhang in front of the sutler's store and staring out into the rain. Cullen rode with Amos Fletcher.

"You've been doing some investigating?" Pickett asked.

"Not much. Haven't had time. Who are you?"

"John. Just call me John."

"Why? You don't have a last name?"

"None that would mean anything."

Meaning, Matt guessed, that just the opposite was true. "What made you give up bounty hunting?"

Pickett decided a little truth wouldn't hurt. "Had a family. Father, mother, brothers, sisters. I was the black sheep. Went out bountyin', catchin' all these bad hombres. Visited home a while back and found there wasn't much left. A bunch had rode through, killed most, raped the rest, didn't leave them much for *minds*. Shock and all that..." He made it sound calm, almost casual, because if he didn't keep an iron grip on himself, he'd scream. As it was, he still moaned and yelled at night, as he had while he was unconscious. Cassie still thought it had something to do with the wounds.

"And you didn't light out after them?"

"No. By the time I'd tended to those that were still living, I'd realized the futility of it all. Something inside of me died...."

"Jesus," breathed Lieutenant Marlowe.

"Almost wish you'd let *me* die, doc."

"I almost wish I had too," Marlowe said. "But where there's life..." He was going to say, "There's hope," but couldn't quite bring himself to say it. "Why don't we let you rest now, John. I can see we've stirred up some memories best left buried."

124

John Pickett nodded and bowed his head. But before they went out the door he raised it and said, "If you see Cassie, could you send her by? She's been a comfort."

He lay back in bed. Luckily he hadn't been carrying any wanted circulars for the Fletcher gang. He'd forgotten about that old Cullen circular.

It could be so easy, he thought. Just let Kincaid know who the hell Fletcher was, what he'd done, how he and his gang were infected. But he wanted Fletcher for himself.

Marlowe and Kincaid strolled together toward the Cohens'. Matt wanted Marlowe to meet the three youngsters.

"Poor man," said Marlowe, "to have your world, your purpose in life, just vanish like that . . ."

"Bull," said Matt. "His world may have vanished, but not his purpose. He didn't give up anything. He's on their trail, you'd better believe that."

Marlowe stared at him. "How do you know that?"

"Number of reasons. I saw his guns hanging up by his bed. I'll bet they've been gone over with rag and oil in the last hour. And most men shot to hell like he was would just die. Not him, though. He wants to live because he's got a purpose. But the real clincher is that I think I know who he might be."

Marlowe turned and stared at Matt, who continued, "A while back, a report came through about a massacre done by some white men in Missouri. Sounded like the one our man there just described. Seems it happened at a place that was named for the family that was massacred—Pickett's Landing. Now, this wouldn't mean a hell of a lot by itself, but I remember hearing of a certain bounty hunter with a scary reputation, name of John Pickett. Pretty well known, he's nailed more than his share of desperadoes. So I think that's who our man is. And I'll tell you, I wouldn't want to be in the shoes of the bastards who raped and killed his family. Something else too. For a man with a purpose like the one he's got, he doesn't seem all that anxious to move on. Not only that, but what was he doing in these parts to begin with?"

Marlowe shrugged, and Matt answered his own question. "I think the bunch he's after are somewhere real close by. . . ."

By this time they had arrived at the Cohens' quarters, where they found not only the three youngsters, but Maggie and Cassie as well.

Matt smiled at Cassie and said, "We were just visiting with

your patient. Looks like you're taking real good care of him—in fact, Mr. Pickett was asking for you."

"How'd you know his name?" exclaimed Cassie.

"Oh, *Cassie*," groaned Maggie.

"Just making sure," said Matt, smiling.

"It's a secret," wailed Cassie.

"It'll stay one," Matt told her.

"He's got his eye on someone," said Maggie, and there was a knowing look in her eye that Matt caught. He'd have to remember to talk to her privately. But for now . . .

"This is Eleanora, doc," he said.

"I thought you said they were *kids*," said Marlowe.

"And Matthew and Enos. Enos is a quiet one."

"I am not," said Enos.

"He's hardly stopped talking since he got back from the latrine," said Maggie. "What did you do to him out there, Matt?"

Matt smiled benignly. "How are you kids feeling? Any better?"

They said they weren't. Matt glanced at Marlowe.

Marlowe shrugged. "Could be just a cold. . . ."

A few minutes later, Matt and Marlowe and Cassie had left the Cohen quarters, Cassie to return to Pickett, Matt to the orderly room to send a wire destined for Pickett's Landing, and Marlowe to the sutler's store to buy a drink.

fifteen ━━━━━━━━━━━

Lieutenant Smaldoon was dug in pretty solidly, commanding what might pass for high ground. Lieutenant Allison and his twenty men blocked the path northward, but that path lay over terrain level with Hungry Buffalo's Cheyenne, so while Hungry Buffalo did his mighty praying, small bands of his warriors tested Mister Allison.

The terrain to the north was level in a general sense but gouged by innumerable cuts and draws and gulches, some of which would run for miles, all part of the High Plains' natural drainage system. Thus the Cheyenne war chiefs would not lead their small bands charging over the high ground, but rather try to slip close along the cracks in the terrain, seeking either isolated victims or weak links in the chain of soldiers.

But the weakness they found was in themselves.

Mr. Allison and Sergeant Chubb, checking the line in the morning, listened courteously to the advice of Corporal Lowenstein.

"We can take 'em easy, sir. With us here and Mr. Smaldoon

up there, and with all the natural cover, we could move in slow and take 'em apart. A lot of 'em just got bows, prob'ly, and they won't be worth diddly after the rain."

Allison frowned slightly and Chubb said, "The bowstrings are gut, sir. If they get wet, they're useless."

Lowenstein continued, "The way it is, sir, we're jes' kinda sittin' ducks. Them Cheyenne keep tryin' these sneaky little maneuvers, creepin' up through the gullies. We got a lot of men that didn't get no sleep last night, sir. Combine that with gettin' soaked yesterday . . ."

Allison said, "In the first place, Corporal, we think most of the Cheyenne *do* have guns. But you have to understand, our mission here is not to kill. These Cheyenne jumped the reservation—shot their way off, yes, but you'd probably have done the same thing if you had the Sanitary Corps coming at you with their needles and the missionaries with their bibles at the same time."

"Needles? You mean they thought the Cheyenne was gonna stand still for havin' *needles* stuck in them?"

"They're going to have to, sooner or later. The white man's got diseases they've never seen before, that can wipe them out. If a white man gets smallpox, there's a good chance he'll live—look at Private Cassidy."

"That where he got all them holes in his face?"

"But for the red man it's certain death."

Lowenstein grimaced. "Poor suckers."

"So we just want to try to keep them from going anywhere, tire 'em out and wait until they realize we're not intending them harm."

"But still, sir, they ain't playin' the same game. They're sneakin' up, tryin' to *kill* us. Ol' Lance Corp Howe, he damn near got his scalp lifted last night. He was cruisin' the line, wakin' fellers up, when a coupla hostiles jumped him. Coulda shot 'im, but they musta wanted to count coup, you know, *axe* 'im. . . ."

"Touchin' ol' Howe, though, is about as easy as grabbin' holda smoke. Y'gotta hand it to 'im, though, sir, he didn't try to shoot 'em. Orders is orders. He jes' started swingin' his piece like an effin' maniac."

Allison was aghast. "Well, for God's sake, man, if it's a question of life or death, start shooting."

"Yeah, well, I figure Howe woulda, sooner or later, but them hostiles give up real quick. Corp Howe was surprised. They didn't fight like Cheyenne usually do."

Chubb frowned, and Allison asked, "What do you think? Could they be running out of food?"

"Mebbe. Wouldn't get that weak that fast, though. Might be somethin' else eatin' at them. Or maybe they sent some youngsters out. You know, chance to count their first coup, somethin' like that."

"All right, Corporal," Allison said, "carry on. Just do your best. Try to keep them penned in, but don't let yourself get killed doing it."

"We'll try, sir. But I got some boys that just understand yes and no. Give 'em a maybe and they'll shoot first and *then* try to figure out if they was in mortal danger. I'd go kinda easy with that 'use your own judgment' stuff, sir, if you don't mind my sayin' so. Lotta these boys ain't got no judgment, they jes' got orders."

Allison and Chubb walked on, slightly crouched, leading their horses. Allison knew and understood the problem. The War Department, in its eagerness to please the public, Congress, and the President, and fill the Western territories with soldiers, wasn't very selective in recruiting. They couldn't afford to be if they expected to fill their quotas. Consequently the average intelligence of a private in the Army of the West wasn't exactly university level. In fact, there were a lot of dumbbells. Not to mention outright criminals, men escaping into the army under assumed names.

Allison sighed. He understood that England shipped its criminals to Australia. He guessed that you could find a function for almost anybody.

"The corporal's right, sir, about givin' these men the choice to shoot or not to shoot."

Allison smiled. To be or not to be. Good classic education, but he could be cold. "Sooner have a dead hostile than a dead private. It's not my job to sacrifice my men for *anything*."

"Ever tell you about takin' Missionary Ridge under Grant and Sheridan? Sheridan was my immediate."

"No, Sergeant, you haven't, but I've read about it. General Grant was not my type of officer. He lost too many men."

"But he was a winner, sir."

Allison nodded grimly. And General McClellan was popular, careful, and a loser. It was a bother. He hoped he was never in a position where he had to order his men forward to probable death.

• • •

Not that his men were the type to take well to such an order. Privates Jackson and Lee, for instance, ex-Rebs, or "galvanized Yankees." They were career privates, and deservedly so. Sleepy-eyed, easy-smiling men, but mean, hard fighters. They didn't take orders well, at least not *Yankee* orders, considering themselves better free-lancers. This herding action ran against their grain. It was possible that some poor Cheyenne woman squatting and peeing would be considered a "hostile foray" by them, and she'd be shot where she squatted, if their rifles could reach that far with any accuracy.

But at this moment their attention was caught by a different kind of "hostile" threat.

"Alvin, did you see what ah thunk ah seed?"

"You mean one of them po', mizzable, gentle Cheyenne, pokin' his feather up outa that far draw?"

"Yeh," drawled Lee, "that's about what ah seed. S'pose it might be a turkey?"

"Le's go take us a look-see."

They got hold of Privates Shortsleeves and Kearney, and along with Lance Corporal Cameron they began to angle off to intercept movement along the far draw.

They didn't take their mounts, since they expected to find the Cheyenne afoot. Some draws were deep enough to conceal horseback riders, but this one wasn't.

They got to the draw and waited for the Cheyenne.

The Cheyenne encampment was beginning to look as though a great battle had already been waged. And lost. Many either lay about or wandered around, weakened by their sickness. Many were coughing, bringing up great gobs of phlegm, and swaying dizzily, the fever upon them and mounting.

Hungry Buffalo was coming to the conclusion that the spot upon which they'd chosen to camp—or been forced to camp—had been the site of some great disaster and the area was permeated with evil spirits, the shades of some mortal enemies—Pawnee, perhaps, or segments of the Snake tribes—and those spirits were laying his people low. Even Hungry Buffalo himself was not feeling well.

But while he came to this conclusion, his small raiding parties still ventured forth.

Crying Eagle, though as ill as any of the rest, had the constitution of a mule, and the temper of one. He insisted on leading a party. He was determined to count coup where others had failed.

He said they would have to leave their horses, since the draw giving closest access was, he knew, too shallow.

They renewed their blue warpaint, he and the four that would go with him—Many Moons, Twin Pines, Painted Calf, and Strong Bow. This last was a warrior stronger than most, whose arrows carried beyond sight and who preferred being called Shadow Maker, though he'd yet to be given that name. They carried war axes, knives, and Spencer repeaters. Strong Bow—whose bow, incidentally, had been dampened and weakened so much that he could throw his arrows farther than he could shoot them—also stuck two feathers in his hair. Crying Eagle disapproved, but said nothing.

They slipped from the camp under careful cover, but as they neared the army line, creeping along a shallow draw, they took fire, heavy fire, slugs licking up clay loam all around them.

While Crying Eagle's faith in the poor marksmanship of the Americans was renewed, he saw no point in hanging around to wait for improvement. He spun and, cursing, led his four men in full retreat.

Lance Corporal Cameron and his men watched them go, frustrated but satisfied. Jackson stood up to watch them disappear. But just then Strong Bow, angry and bitter, glanced back over his shoulder and saw Jackson standing. Strong Bow stopped, spun, threw his Spencer to his shoulder, and shot.

Jackson cried out as the slug nicked his shoulder.

Private Lee, enraged, then leaped to his feet and took off down the draw after the Cheyenne. That bastard wasn't going to shoot his buddy and get away with it.

Crying Eagle had heard the shot, turned, seen Strong Bow running after him, grinning, and, far behind him, Private Lee in pursuit.

He also heard Cameron bawling, "Lee, goddammit, get your ass back here!"

Crying Eagle waved Strong Bow by, and then ran after him for a while. Dodging around a crook in the draw, though, leaving Lee's sight, he suddenly turned off, climbing and diving into the high grass flanking the draw. He would ambush the American. He grew almost dizzy with excitement. Sweat ran down his forehead, stinging his eyes, blurring his vision.

Then the American rounded into sight, high-stepping down the draw.

Spotted Hawk saw he would not have to shoot him. He could leap upon him as he passed, destroy him with his war axe, and thereby count coup. If no other Americans showed, he would whistle the rest back to hack up the body and also count coup.

The American got closer. He could see Lee's tongue hanging out.

Crying Eagle gathered himself . . . and jumped!

Once Lance Corporal Cameron found out that Jackson had only been nicked, he really started cursing. He saw Lee disappear. Then he thought he heard a war cry, or something like it.

But then he didn't hear anything for the longest time. Thirty seconds, but it seemed an eternity.

Then he heard a shot, cursed, stood up, and started trotting down the draw with Shortsleeves, Kearney, and Jackson at his heels.

They rounded the crook in the draw, beyond which Crying Eagle had hidden, and saw, up ahead, Private Lee standing over a body. Drawing closer, they saw that Lee had a strange expression on his face.

They got there and looked down at Crying Eagle, who was lying on his side, his axe beside him, fallen from an open, lax hand. His breathing was labored.

Corporal Cameron crouched and circled Crying Eagle. "Where the hell did you hit him?"

"Ah didn't hit 'im at all," drawled Lee. "He jumped at me from up there. Scared the livin' crap outa me . . . jes' for a second, though. Ah jumps and he sails by, lands right there where he's lyin'."

"Busted somethin'?"

"Nothin' ah could find. He's burnin' up somethin' fierce, though."

"Then what was that goddamn shot?"

"Jes' wanted you fellers to hurry on along."

Corporal Cameron glared at him, then shifted his gaze to Crying Eagle, squatting down to get a closer look. Crying Eagle looked squarely into his eyes, but Cameron could swear the Indian didn't see him.

Cameron stood up. "No one go near him," he said in a voice that prohibited argument. "You touched him?"

"Ah *tol'* you ah did," said Lee.

"Okay, you jes' stand clear, by yourself. Now, how many diseases you had? Y'know, mumps, measles?"

"Had 'em all. 'Cept pox. This ain't pox, is it?"

"Don' know. It's *somethin'*. Kearney, you move your ass

like the goddamn wind, get Chubb an' Allison here."

Eight minutes later, Allison and Chubb came riding down the draw, throwing caution to the winds but ready to dive from their mounts.

They dismounted, and Cameron threw up a salute and filled them both in, wasting no words.

"Have you seen anything like it, Sergeant?"

"I seen the works, sir, an' this is one of them . . . I think."

Allison eyed him askance. "We'd better get him back to the post fast. Doc Marlowe'll know what it is. If it's just this beggar with a bad cold, that's not so bad, but if it's something contagious . . ."

"Lee's already touched him, sir," said Cameron, "but he says he's already had everything they is."

"'Ceptin' pox, sir, ah ain't had pox."

Pox. Allison stared down at Crying Eagle. If there was a chance this was pox . . .

"Cassidy's had pox," Lee practically screamed.

Allison decided. "Go get Cassidy, Kearney. Bring him and three horses. Lee, you and Cassidy will take this Indian down to the post, get him to Doc Marlowe. If it *is* pox, Marlowe will know what to do for you. If it's *not* pox, and Cassidy catches whatever it is, it won't be something that can't be cured."

Cassidy, when he heard that, wasn't so sure. "What if it's something that neither of us ever heard of, sir?"

"You get going, soldier, or you'll get something that you *have* heard of. And even if he dies on the way, take him on in to Marlowe."

"Yessir." Cassidy turned to Lee. "Grab his feet."

"Me?!"

133

sixteen

Billie hadn't had much luck. Stretch Dobbs had been about the closest she'd come to nailing a soldier. Hattie and Aggie had been luckier. Some soldiers had gotten drunk one night and slipped into the stables to take turns with the two girls. Billie had been outside the post at the time, servicing Ray Cullen, the hatchet-faced man who never got enough. Just her luck.

The next day she'd approached the five privates who'd been with Hattie and Aggie, but they seemed to have had enough. In fact, once they'd taken good, sober looks at the girls in the full light of day, they'd decided they'd had more than enough and commenced worrying their dumb heads off. And they couldn't get clear of Billie fast enough.

But then, early one morning, about the time Crying Eagle was collapsing, Billie lucked onto the incorrigibly horny Private Jeff Dow. How she'd missed Dow for so long, or vice versa, the Lord only knew.

Dow's mouth twisted into a kind of grin. He liked Billie's

shape and attitude, and to hell with the rest—his face had been splotchy too, when he was a kid. He thought she stank a bit too, but in the stables, who could tell where the stink was coming from?

Astride Billie, half-buried in sawdust—and probably manure, though they looked for the cleanest spot—Dow's thoughts wandered to the widow.

The widow was okay in the sack, but kind of ladylike. She should cut loose once in a while, like this gal. . . .

"What'd you say your name was?"

"Billie. What's yours?"

"Diamond," he said, grinning. "Jack Diamond."

A while later they came out of the stables, Dow hauling her out before she was completely dressed. He grinned for everyone to see, but no one was watching.

In fact, no one seemed to care what he did, not even Sergeant Cohen. Cohen had looked at him that morning, raised his eyebrows, but hadn't said a damned thing.

To hell with it. Let him wait. He still had two days. He'd let Cohen wait until the last moment before telling him. The bastard had put him on one too many details to get any favors from *him*. The fact that he'd had much of the previous two weeks free of duty seemed to have made no lasting impression on Dow. He decided to go see the widow.

Dow headed for the paddock, with Billie following. The U.S. Army Remount Service had herded in threescore the day before, hoping to exchange a number, disappointed to find many of the mounts gone. There were close to sixty horses milling about the paddock.

Billie thought it was fun the way Dow got the horses running around as he picked one out.

Dow made a show of being selective, but they were all about the same—big bay geldings. He was just showing off. He knew as much about horseflesh as he did about communicable diseases. Cows he knew, from his youth, and he knew draft horses had to be big, but good horseflesh? Didn't matter; he mistreated any he took.

Dow saddled the bay, and with scarcely a nod for Billie, he rode off.

Billie stayed with the horses, just inside the paddock, watching them. She'd had a dream once, of a fine house and a stable of spirited horses. But that was before she realized her family was dirt-poor and getting poorer. And before Fletcher and his excitement came along. This paddock was probably as close as she was ever going to get to that stable.

Cassie Smaldoon and John Pickett walked beneath the overhang, heading from their quarters to the stable and paddock. They could have angled across the parade, but Pickett preferred not to. He didn't want Fletcher to see him, even though there was no real danger—nobody circulated flyers showing the hunter, just the hunted.

"You're doing just fine," said Cassie. "Coming right along. Pretty soon you'll have all your strength back, and then you can—" A thought had popped into her head and she blushed.

Pickett noticed it and threw in a limp and a stagger to confound her. He already had all his strength back, but he had no time or space in his mind for thoughts of love.

"Hope the remount service didn't take *my* horse," he said. It too was a bay gelding, but it had distinctive markings on its head and hind legs. It also had dependable strength and endurance that had enabled Pickett to ride down many an outlaw.

They reached the paddock and encountered a wild scene. Billie had decided to play with the horses like a kid, get them running around the way Dow had done. Which she had, but beyond her wildest dreams. The horses were practically stampeding around the paddock, with Billie trapped in the center.

Cassie and Pickett watched, Cassie excited, Pickett with eyes narrowed. Cassie liked horses and worked fearlessly with them. She would have enjoyed being in Billie's shoes. "Isn't it *glorious*, John?" she exulted.

Billie didn't think it was glorious, though. She was scared. She wanted to get out. And when she thought she saw an opening, she made a dash for the fence.

But that only spooked the horses further, and one careened into her, knocking her down.

The horses ran right by her now, some leaping over, others just skirting her. Fear kept her still.

Cassie started over the fence, but Pickett took her arm in a viselike grip, stopping her cold.

The force of his grip shocked her.

Pickett looked up for one of the guards. Unless they were sleeping, one of them should have noticed something.

They had. Three had, and they all looked down, probably betting on how long Billie would last.

"Go get the boss of this bunch," Pickett yelled up at them. "Tell him one of his gals is about to get trampled to death."

The guards seemed not to hear him and, with a curse, Pickett leaped over the paddock railing.

Two of the guards ran for help.

Pickett ducked and dodged his way to where the girl lay. Then he stood over her, waving his arms at the onrushing horses, which easily swerved to miss him and the girl.

The horses began to slow. Pickett saw Fletcher climbing over the paddock railing, in no hurry at all, and sauntering out to join them.

"Goddammit, get up, Billie," Fletcher ordered.

Billie did so, and Amos Fletcher took her by the elbow and led her to the fence, the horses now only trotting about, some having already stopped.

Pickett followed Fletcher and the girl to the fence, where Fletcher scowled at Pickett. "You're so brave, whyn't *you* haul her out?"

Pickett saw Cassie starting to open her mouth, and he glared at her, saying, "I've been sick. It's hard enough standing up out there, much less haulin' a dead weight. I didn't know she was only scared."

Fletcher didn't say anything, just grabbed Billie by the elbow and took her away.

Meanwhile, short-timer Jeff Dow rode into the widow Bennett's yard, alive with lust. The session with Billie had only whetted his appetite. He was springing from the saddle when he saw Jack Diamond coming out of the barn.

"What the hell are *you* doing here? This is my—"

"I've been finishing some repairs I started," said Diamond quietly, coming up to him.

"Well, who the hell said you could just waltz over here an', an'—"

Diamond was now looming over him, not looking the slightest bit apologetic.

The widow appeared just then. "Oh, Jeff, Mr. Diamond showed up and insisted on doing the work. I didn't ask him to. He just . . . started working."

The widow was drawn to Diamond, but at the same time he seemed too implacable. With Jeff there was a chance she could use her body to get him to do things, bend him to her will, but Diamond seemed resolutely his own man, impossible to get close to. Of course she was wrong on both counts, but she was a desperate woman. She didn't have many years left to catch a good man, and with Naomi growing up so fast, anybody coming by would only have eyes for her.

No, Jeff Dow seemed her best bet, and she figured she'd better grab while she could. "Come on inside, Jeff. Let Mr. Diamond finish what he's doing."

Jeff Dow strode into the sod house as though he owned it. He soon *would* own it, he thought with satisfaction.

The widow followed him in. He went into the kitchen but she stopped in the door. "Why don't we . . . adjourn to the bedroom, Jeff?" She carefully arranged her face into a seductive expression.

Dow stared at her. "Do what? Uh-jurn? What the hell's that?"

"Oh, c'mon, Jeff, *you* know. Come into the bedroom."

"Where's Naomi?"

"Out in the barn, watching Mr. Diamond."

Impossible, thought Jeff. She would have run to greet him.

"Or off riding her horse. She won't bother us."

Jeff Dow figured it was time to get back at her. Besides, he'd just gotten some. His pecker was hardly dry. Let the widow suffer some, let *her* feel frustrated for a while.

"I don't think so, Zelly. We had an agreement, remember? Anyway, not now. At least not while Diamond's around."

"He's in the barn."

"I don' know, Zelly. To be truthful, can't say as how I feel like it just now. You know how that is."

The widow stared at him in disbelief—and in some fear. Was he going to escape her, elude her grasp?

"Jeff," she said huskily, "I need you, *now*."

He just smiled. "You hang onto that thought, Zelly. I'm gonna take me a little stroll around the property."

And he walked on out of the sod house, leaving the widow sorely frustrated and extremely anxious. But she was not a stupid woman; partially blind to his flaws, but not stupid. And she sensed that this was not just a ploy on Jeff's part, that there was more to it. Perhaps he had another woman hidden away somewhere.

Jeff Dow wandered past the barn, hearing the loud hammering. His lips tightened. He was sorry he'd ever brought Diamond by, the interfering bastard.

He strolled along the line dividing the corn-seeded northwest forty from the plowed southwest.

He stopped at the edge of the property and looked to the east. It was all good land, dammit, land a man with ambition could stretch out and grow on. Once he got hold of the widow's money, he could buy more land, get some cattle, maybe hire some boys to do the actual work.

He shook his head, wondering at the dirty work he'd put into this courtship. Was the widow worth it? He thought of her back in the house, going crazy with frustration, and smiled. He knew how to handle women like her.

He looked up. And the scarecrow, Arnold Bennett, looked back down at him.

"Arnold," he said, "you're as worthless out here as you ever was. But, ol' timer, your days are done."

And he suddenly yanked out his Scoffs and started pumping lead into the scarecrow.

The scarecrow twitched and jerked for a while, but finally, as Jeff's guns emptied, it collapsed in a tangle of sticks and torn cloth.

Diamond had stuck his head out of the barn to see what was going on, wondering where he'd left his own Scoffs.

And the widow had run out in the yard, alarmed, afraid that Jeff and Mr. Diamond were going at it.

But when she saw what had happened, she was enraged. Absolutely furious. The widow *honored* the memory of her late husband.

She saw Jeff Dow jauntily returning, scattering empties and reloading as he came. She turned and ran back into the house.

Jack Diamond silently watched Jeff Dow saunter by, failing to understand. He'd surmised what the scarecrow represented, a half-respectful, half-derisive memorial to Bennett, but either way meaningful. Jeff Dow had to have a head full of rocks.

Diamond saw Naomi riding toward the house from the distance. A girl ought not to go out riding by herself like that, but he had to admit she rode well.

Jeff Dow entered the sod house. The kitchen was empty. He went to the closed bedroom door, smiling in anticipation. But it was locked.

"Zelly? You in there? Zelly?"

"Go away," she said from within. The words had a strangled, croaking sound.

"Zelly, lemme in. We gotta talk. We gotta *plan*. We gotta . . . *do* things. Hell's bells, gal, a few minutes ago you was all hot an' bothered. . . .

"That scarecrow warn't worth shit, Zelly, warn't doin' the

139

corn no good. Corn don't grow up here, didn't dumb Arnold know that? Zelly? You gonna come out? You gonna say anything?"

He waited, but there was no reply.

"I'm warnin' you, Zelly, you better make up your mind."

Silence. And Jeff Dow, a volatile man who was now feeling incredible pangs of lust, went a bit crazy. "Goddammit, if you ain't comin' out, I'm comin' in."

He ran at the door, and bounced off. Arnold may not have built much else well, but he'd fashioned some solid doors.

Jeff Dow renewed his attack. Either the door would go or his shoulder would, goddammit. But he was wrong. As he launched himself forward for another go at it, he ran into an immovable forearm possessing the size and strength of an oak limb.

Jeff whirled to face Diamond, who, despite the action he'd taken, was expressionless. Jeff's immediate reaction was to reach for his guns.

"You do that and I'll take 'em and ram 'em up your ass," Diamond warned him, and he believed it.

"Now I'll give you a little advice," Diamond went on quietly. "You lay off that door, and lay off that woman. She's a lady. You treat her like one or I'll break you in two." Diamond smiled—a sinister one, considering the context. "Do I make myself clear?"

Jeff thought about it. Then he backed off a safe distance and started shouting. "You sure do make yourself clear, Diamond. An' somethin' else is clear too. You done lost yourself a husband, Zelly. I'll be goddamned if I ever come back to this place, thanks to this pile of shit."

And he turned and raced from the house.

Naomi had ridden up and heard the tail end of the encounter. She yelled at Jeff as he mounted his horse, "Wait, Jeff, wait!"

But he didn't wait. He rode on out of the yard. Naomi looked around to see Diamond looming in the doorway, a thunderous expression on his face.

Naomi turned away, mounted her own horse, and took off after Dow. Diamond watched, his face now thoughtful.

Finally the sound of hoofbeats had receded to silence, and the only sounds were the tiny, muffled sobs of the widow Bennett.

Naomi caught up to Dow easily, but he'd slowed to wait for her.

140

"Your ma, Naomi," he said as she rode up "she about drives me nuts. An' thet Diamond . . ."

"I *hate* him," she said, her young breasts heaving. "But Ma, she needs you, Jeff. And *I* need you."

"You need me?" he said softly. "How much do you need me, Naomi?" The time had come. "Answer . . . *woman*."

Naomi said nothing. She was flattered at being called a woman, and sometimes she felt like one, but she wondered what came next, what it involved. What was she supposed to say? Or do?

Jeff Dow dismounted and then drew her from her horse.

He led her to a nearby draw. The horses remained where they were, contentedly beginning to graze.

Jeff Dow looked Naomi up and down, and she in turn regarded him with large, luminous, wondering eyes. She was about to *know*. . . .

Slowly, Dow stripped the clothing from her, trying to control his breathing. God, his head was bursting. He thought he might even pass out.

It got worse, the more the girl's body was bared—the taut breasts, the flat stomach, the hard, compact buttocks, the fine down over her sex, golden and silky. . . .

At that time, if anyone had told Jeff Dow that he was carrying a highly infectious and destructive disease, and that it was passed primarily through sex, he wouldn't have cared one whit. He probably wouldn't have given a damn at any time, even at his most accommodating, but then and there, tearing his own uniform off, it wouldn't have made one bit of difference. He was oblivious to all but the body that was sinking to the sandy loam beneath him.

He was poised, ready to enter her, when he happened to glance up and found himself staring down the barrel of Diamond's .45-caliber Scoff.

"On your feet, scum," said Diamond in a tight voice Dow had never heard, and he obeyed instantly.

"Now get dressed."

Still under the gun, he threw his clothes on.

"Now ride."

Dow sensed that if Diamond blew up just then, the entire Territory of Wyoming would go with him.

Dow ran to his horse, mounted in a flash, and rode off. He might have thrown a shot back, but he knew, if he missed killing him, that Diamond would hunt him forever. He just rode, and rode hard.

"Get dressed, girl," said Diamond, eyes averted.

"You bastard," she hissed, suddenly very grown up. "Take a look, why don't you, you bastard. . . ."

But Diamond refused, and finally she dressed.

On the way back to the house, Diamond adjusted his thinking about Naomi. She wasn't an innocent little kid. He probably should have let Dow have her. It probably wasn't even her first time.

By the time they'd reached the house, Naomi's anger had hardened into silent hate, and what she showed was keen embarrassment.

But when they reached the widow, waiting outside the house, Diamond said nothing of what had happened. "Reckon I'll just go finish up what I started," he said, dismounting and heading for the barn.

Naomi disappeared into the house.

The widow, seeing that no one was going to explain anything to her, settled for moaning, "I've *lost* him, lost the only man I had a chance for." She saw that Diamond had disappeared into the barn and yelled after him, "Damn you! Why'd you ever have to come here?"

seventeen

Back at Outpost Number Nine, Matt Kincaid had just finished oiling his guns—the Scoff for his left hand, but a Peacemaker for his right—when a knock came on the door of his quarters. He called out, "Enter," and Eleanora Culloch came in.

She looked beautiful. She wore a wan, pale look that fit her bone structure, and her face was prettily flushed.

Matt got up and stepped toward her. Which was fortunate, because he was close enough to catch her when she fell.

Picking her up, he felt the fever, right through her thin cotton dress.

He put her on his bed and felt her forehead. Like the top of a stove. This girl was *sick*.

Matt snatched her up and ran from his quarters. He dashed across the parade carrying the girl, hardly aware of the weight. He headed for the enlisted day room, for Lieutenant Marlowe.

Privates Malone and Dobbs watched him run. "Lookit what Matt done to thet pore girl," said Stretch. "That man's *death* on women, near as much a killer as me."

"Marlowe!" Matt roared, and Stretch and Malone jumped back a pace. Marlowe shot from the day room like a frightened deer.

"What's wrong?!" he exclaimed.

"She's on fire, Doc. Came to me and passed out."

"Lay her down."

"I'll take her inside," said Matt. "No troub—"

"Lay her down!"

Matt laid her down on the parade, and Marlowe went down on his knees by her side, saying as he went, "I've already got weak people in there. I'm not exposing them to something new."

He carefully examined Eleanora. First, of course, he noted the fever. He opened the eyes and saw watery redness. He also saw that her nasal passages seemed congested.

"Wonder how long she's been like this?"

"She and the other kids have been complaining of weakness ever since we found them," Matt said.

"Should have seen this last night," said Marlowe. He opened her mouth, peeled back the lips, and found bluish-white specks surrounded by bright red areas.

"Damn," he groaned.

Then he found the rash, which usually began at the hairline. It was there, and behind the ears, on the forehead, on the neck, and on down the body.

"Measles," Marlowe said.

Matt stared at him, silent, but only because his thoughts were racing too fast for expression. He recalled everything connected with the girl, including the wagon train with its mysteriously bedridden occupants.

Captain Conway and Sergeant Cohen came up now, in time to hear Marlowe's diagnosis.

"We definitely can't put her in there," said Marlowe, meaning the enlisted day room.

"Officers' day room," said Warner Conway. Then he turned and roared at the men who were slowly closing in, "Anybody who's had measles—that's *measles*, and you're *sure* of it— step forward. The rest of you stay the hell away!"

Most of the men edged forward, the rest scattered.

"Hold it!" shouted Warner Conway, struck by a thought. "Any of you that haven't had it but have had contact with these three kids, you look up Lieutenant Marlowe first thing."

"You, you, and you," said Sergeant Cohen, "get this girl

144

into the officer's day room and fix up a bed. The doc'll go with you."

"All of you had it?" asked Marlowe, looking around, and Conway, Kincaid, Cohen, and Fox all nodded. "That's a break," said Marlowe.

"Not much of one," said Matt, and they looked at him. "I've been giving it some thought, and unless I miss my guess, that wagon train was loaded with measles."

"This girl will be awfully sick, but she'll recover," Marlowe said. "But measles is practically death to an Indian. System can't handle it at all. Measles itself doesn't kill, like cholera, but it weakens them so much they catch everything else, usually pneumonia or something like that, and that *does* kill."

"So we've probably got a tribe of Cheyenne out there getting very sick."

"Probably dying by now," said Captain Conway. "That rain we had, that cold rain..."

And never were prophets so honored, for at that moment the main gate swung open and Privates Lee and Cassidy rode in, the horse between them bearing the still living flesh that was Crying Eagle.

Lee and Cassidy almost bolted when they saw the doctor and the other officers running at them.

Marlowe, knowing what to look for, took five seconds to diagnose. "He's got it, and likely pneumonia's killing him. Get him into that day room."

"What *is* it?" cried Cassidy.

"Measles."

Lee and Cassidy both broke out in wide grins.

Captain Conway was going to yell at them, but then he understood what they were grinning about. "You men are to be commended for taking a chance like that, bringing this man down here."

"Thank you, suh," said Lee, but Cassidy grumped, "Didn't have no goddamn choice."

Everybody hustled around, converting the officers' day room into a full-fledged hospital ward.

John Pickett watched with interest from his window, absent-mindedly snapping his heavy Colts out and back into their holsters. His gaze shifted to the sutler's store, where Fletcher and his gang were also watching.

The door suddenly opened and Cassie burst in. "John. I

145

won't be able to see you much. There's measles. The kids have it, Eleanora and Matthew and Enos, and they think the Cheyenne have it. Matt's going out to try to get to the Cheyenne and help them. But I have to go help in the day room. I've had measles."

"So have I. Let's go."

Jeff Dow rode in just then. "What's going on?"

"Measles," said Private Hurley. "If you've had it, you can head for the day room and pitch in. But if you haven't, then you better stay clear. You had it?"

Dow had had it but said, "No I haven't."

"You and me both. Maybe we'll ride with Matt."

"Whaddya mean?"

"He's takin' a patrol out."

"What for?"

"If he don't catch the Cheyenne, they'll prob'ly die. They got the measles too."

"Good. Let 'em die, good riddance."

Hurley gave Dow a look, then turned and walked away. If there was one sure way to waste time, it was talking to Dow. "Hey, buddy," Dow yelled after him, "I am too short to worry about all this crap."

Besides which, Dow had enough to worry about—how to get back into the widow's good graces, how to handle that effin' Diamond. He wondered if Diamond or Naomi had told the widow about what had happened . . . or *almost* happened. Chances were, knowing the way Diamond liked to pussyfoot around things, she didn't know.

But *Diamond* . . . that bastard had his goddamn nerve, pulling a gun on him. He'd have to get him for that one. He decided he'd have to give it some thought, sleep on it.

The day room was just about converted. All they needed now were patients. Matt had delayed his departure, partly to see that the kids, off in one corner, were being taken care of properly, partly because there was no sense in going in the middle of the night, and partly trying to decide who to take. It meant assembling a patrol comprised of measles-immune men, which gave an easy out to anyone who didn't care to go up against the Cheyenne, sick or otherwise. Matt noted just who had helped fix up the day room.

In the meantime, Ben Cohen was having his problems—with the widow Bennett, of all people.

The widow had panicked and ridden for the post, determined to reclaim her man. Naomi had ridden with her, trailed by Jack Diamond, who had scowled the whole way. It was not a pleasant ride for any of them.

Once on post, they'd heard about the measles. Naomi had had it, so Giselle volunteered her for the nursing detachment, which Naomi didn't mind, since it meant she'd be around all those nice men.

Diamond had trudged off for the barracks, where he ignored Dow, who'd decided to play it like nothing had ever happened.

That left Giselle on her own. She heard that a patrol was being formed to head out after the Cheyenne. Brave Jeff, hurt as he was by her treatment, was sure to volunteer for the patrol. Why, he might even decide to reenlist. She *had* to stop that.

Inevitably, she ended up in Sergeant Cohen's orderly room.

"Sergeant, you simply *can't* send Private Dow out on any dangerous missions. He's so close to getting out of the service, and we've made so many plans."

"I wasn't—"

"The thing is, we had a little tiff. I wasn't just afraid you'd send him out on patrol, but that the poor dear might volunteer."

"Dow?"

"Or that he might even reenlist!"

"The army's not *that* bad, Mrs. Bennett."

"Oh, I didn't mean that. I just meant that I could give him so much more."

"Yeah, well, save your breath, Mrs. Bennett. I wasn't planning to send Dow out on any patrols or anything. If he re-ups, that's his business, and that'd change things, but the way it stands now—"

Flora Conway entered. "Sergeant Cohen," she began, but then she saw the widow Bennett. "Oh, Mrs. Bennett, you're here. Good. Are you having any luck?" Without waiting for a reply, she said to Cohen, "Sergeant, you simply can't send this private out on patrol where he might get hurt or killed. He's too close to being discharged, isn't he?"

Ben Cohen had all the respect in the world for Flora Conway, but he sure as hell didn't like being pressured, by *anyone*.

Then Maggie marched in. "I see you two beat me here," she said. "Is Ben being agreeable?"

147

"Meaning no disrespect, ladies," said Sergeant Cohen to Flora and Maggie, "but do either of you two *know* this Dow?"

"The widder's over there tryin' to save your tender ass, Dow," said Private Coyne. "Tryin' to keep you from gettin' killed, tryin' to get you special treatment."

Dow sat up on his bunk. "What? The hell you say."

"That's the straight of it."

"Well hell, *I* didn't ask her for no help."

"I think the captain's lady's in there too."

"Jesus wept."

"An' I saw Maggie Cohen go in, besides."

"Aw, hell," groaned Dow, "with all that pressure bein' put on Cohen—*you* know effin' *Cohen*—he'll be sure to send me. And goddammit, I ain't so certain I wouldn't be glad to go. To hell with the widder."

But Cohen had resisted the temptation to reverse himself just to show he couldn't be pressured. "I'm not saying I wouldn't ever pay attention to any advice you ladies might have to offer, but I'd decided a long time ago that I wasn't going to risk Dow's ass—errr, life—this close to discharge."

Just then, Dow himself entered. "Hey, Sarge, I don't like this pressure any more than you do, and I didn't ask for it."

"Ladies," said Sergeant Cohen, "this is Private Dow."

"You got your nerve, Zelly," said Dow, ignoring Flora and Maggie. Then, to Sergeant Cohen: "Sarge, whyn't you jes' sign me up fer that patrol anyway. I've *had* the measles."

Cohen's eyes narrowed. "Why weren't you helping in the day room?"

"Aw, come on, Sarge," said Dow ingratiatingly.

Cohen regarded him coldly. "I've had about enough of you, Private. You're not going on any patrol. Now get out of here."

Dow grabbed hold of the widow and unceremoniously hauled her out of the orderly room. Once outside, he said, "See the trouble you've made for me?"

"I'm sorry, Jeff. I was only trying to help. I was so sorry about what happened back home . . . I shouldn't have locked you out . . . I was afraid you'd do something foolish."

"Sorry, huh?" He grinned. "Okay, show 'me how sorry." He figured many eyes were on him and the widow. "Come on." He started leading her away.

"Where are we going?"

"The stables. I got me my own special little patch. You can show me how sorry there."

She understood. And stopped dead.

"Goddammit," he croaked, "come *on*." He was being shamed right in front of the men.

The widow stared at him, blood draining from her face. "Please, Jeff, let's go home. There's plenty of time for that."

The ladies had left the orderly room, and Cohen had drifted to the door, where he kept an eye on Dow and the widow. He didn't understand what was going on.

"Then to hell with you," sneered Dow, and turned and marched toward the sutler's store, yelling, "Billie!"

Billie emerged, smiled at Dow, and said, "Well, hello there, Jack Diamond."

Dow almost crapped and Diamond, standing some distance away, wasn't sure he was hearing right.

Dow grabbed hold of Billie roughly and led her toward the stables.

The widow turned away, biting her lip, and Maggie was there to lead her into the Cohen quarters.

There was little admiration around the parade for Dow, the prevalent thought being that a man with only a day or two left could get away with *anything*.

Jack Diamond was simply angry, and perplexed by the widow, but Cohen was enraged. He'd finally caught on and felt like walking into the stables and beating the crap out of Dow, which he could do with his goddamn pinkie alone. But he wouldn't soil himself that way. Instead, he stomped back into the orderly room and sent for Lieutenant Kincaid.

Captain Conway, vaguely aware of what was happening, said, "I think I could probably discharge him right now. Extraordinary circumstances."

Cohen glared at Conway. "What I'd really like," he grated, "would be for him to re-up. Then I'd kill the bastard."

Matt Kincaid walked in.

"Matt," Cohen said, "do me a favor. Take Allison's first squad. Most have had the measles. Fill it out with some others. But make sure Dow goes."

"Be a pleasure." Matt had heard what had happened. "Be leaving in about fifteen minutes." He then sent for Squad Leader Hicks from Allison's platoon.

But not five minutes later, before Hicks had arrived, Mrs. Bennett was back in the orderly room; it didn't take any time at all for the news to get around.

"I've heard you're sending Private Dow, Sergeant."

"Yep."

"Please reconsider. This has been an awful day. Jeff's not in his right mind."

"You know what he's doin' right now?"

She nodded miserably. "But he's young and confused. I'm sure I could help him. And he's different when he's home with me."

Cohen stared at her. "Don't you ever give up? What the hell does it take to make you give up?"

Widow Bennett thought about it. "Not some momentary lapse. One must forgive those moments for the good that's in people. And you, Sergeant, have been putting poor Jeff under terrible pressure, trying to get him to reenlist."

So it was Cohen who, with a despairing glance at Matt, gave up. "Okay, okay. Matt, drop him from the patrol, would you?" Matt nodded. "And Captain Conway, sir," he called into the CO's office, "could you sign the discharge? I'll draw up the papers."

Ben Cohen looked at the widow. "You've got your wish, Mrs. Bennett, but I have to tell you that your desperate need for a man is blinding you."

"You're probably right, Sergeant, but I always have had to learn things the hard way."

But the hardest was yet to come. When Matt's patrol finally saddled up—ten men, most of them from Allison's first squad—an eleventh, Dow, was with them.

"You don't have to go," said Sergeant Cohen dully.

"I'm goin', Sarge. Sign me up for another three years. And all these here men are witnesses."

Cohen nodded but didn't say a word. There was a gleam in his eye, though.

He was aware of the widow standing near him, a stricken look on her face. He murmured, "Count yourself lucky, ma'am. I'm the one that's getting the shaft."

He happened to glance up, and caught the mounted Jack Diamond watching the widow. Diamond's eyes shifted to Cohen. And then Diamond slowly shook his head.

Cohen wasn't sure what he meant.

The patrol rode out.

A little while later, Marlowe finished his rounds and staggered to the sutler's store for a pick-me-up. Once again the Fletcher gang was present. Marlowe wondered which girl the private had taken to the stables.

Suddenly he was alert, his tiredness vanished. The measles had set him thinking about other diseases.

These women . . . if the soldiers had been playing around with them, then . . .

One of the girls was leaning against the rough pine bar of the sutler's store. Marlowe steeled himself, wandered over, and slouched against the bar next to her. "Glass of beer, Pop," he ordered, and Pop Evans stared at him. Marlowe usually drank only the best whiskey, reserved for the officers of Easy.

But he brought him the beer.

Marlowe grinned at the girl, who was Aggie. She leered back at him.

"I'm so goddamn tired," groaned Marlowe, and he raised the glass to his lips, taking a deep swallow. Then, as if exhibiting his weariness, he let his hand and the glass slam down hard beside where Aggie was resting her arm on the bar.

The glass shattered while still in his hand. Marlowe cut himself—not badly, and he'd been thoughtful enough to slam the glass down with his off-hand, the left—but also managed to slash Aggie's arm. Blood leaked from them both and mingled. Marlowe started swabbing and sopping it all up with his bandanna, and then said, "Fortunately, I'm a doctor. Come on, young lady, I'll have that patched up in no time."

Which is how, with action beyond the call of duty, Marlowe got himself not only a blood sample but the living host herself. There was no telling what random scrapings might turn up, what close examination might reveal.

eighteen

Lieutenant Marlowe stayed up the entire night, searching for what ailed Aggie and her confederates. A small lab was set up in a corner of Matt Kincaid's office. Marlowe was trying to keep all the diseases separate, and Conway had told him to use Matt's office. There he examined blood samples under his microscope, scraped samples from various parts of Aggie's body and examined them. . . .

Aggie, away from the influence of Fletcher, turned out to be a frightened and willing subject for study. Marlowe got all the cooperation he needed.

It was time-consuming. No way had yet been invented to identify the spirochete that carried syphilis, so the only way to diagnose the disease was to eliminate other possibilities through exhaustive tests.

But so much had been written about the signs and symptoms of syphilis that by the time morning arrived, he was pretty sure it *was* syphilis. There was one other test he could try, not very conclusive but worth a shot. The disease sometimes responded positively to doses of potassium iodide. Not very effective, but better than nothing, and certainly better than mercury; Marlowe had read of cases where the victims preferred syphilis to being smeared with mercury, and there were innumerable case histories on file attributing death to mercury poisoning. Marlowe had some of just about every medication known to science in his medical bag, and he fed Aggie a dose. Then he put her to bed on a cot in Matt's office and told her to stay there. It was morning by then, and Captain Conway, Lieutenant Fox, and Sergeant Cohen were checking in. He filled them in on what was happening, though he cautiously did not give them his tentative conclusions, and then went off and crawled into a bedroll on the floor of one of the Sanitary Corps wagons.

He fell asleep dreaming uncomfortably of Syphilus, the fictional hero of a Latin poem. The poem had been written in 1530 by the Italian physician Girolamo Fracastoro. It was a poem about the disease, which then came to be known by the name of the poem's hero.

And just before he went under, he remembered St. Dionysius and St. Minus, the sixteenth-century patron saints of syphilitics.

Meanwhile, Matt's patrol was nearing its objective.

They'd selected mounts from among the new remount horses and had ridden steadily, if not hard, through the night. Private Lee, dog-tired but game, had ridden with them. He was anxious to get back to his buddy, Jackson. And he was also able to tell them about how far they yet had to go. He was wrong.

Unknown to Lee, Matt, and the rest of the patrol, but also unknown to Smaldoon and Allison to the north, Hungry Buffalo had picked his Cheyenne up during the night, and moved south.

Hungry Buffalo had decided that the location, the expedition, *something* about the whole affair, was a plague upon his people. They had to move. They'd go back to the reservation if they had to, back east through Cutter's Gap, but first they'd try the south. There were no Americans waiting for them there, as far as they knew.

The night they moved out was the night of a late moon, and they were gone by the time the moon rose. It was about 2:00 A.M. when both Smaldoon and Allison were roused from sleep by night sentries, who reported that the Cheyenne had vanished.

Smaldoon, Allison, and the NCOs conferred. "East or

south," said Allison. "You go south, Clay, you know the land, and I'll go east."

With dawn, Matt spread his patrol out in combat formation, a couple of diamonds, with Dow and Private Ives riding point.

"We ain't nowhere near, suh," pointed out Lee, but Matt only nodded. He'd been caught unprepared before in his career—not often, but it had happened. But it wasn't going to happen again.

And as it happened, Dow, on the left point, ran into a forward patrol of Cheyenne. He yelped and rode back toward Matt, who was centered in the formation.

By then, Matt too had glimpsed the Cheyenne. He thought they were riding their horses in curiously tentative fashion, but maybe it was just the distance and his imagination.

He saw the Cheyenne turn their horses and retreat. Not a very feisty bunch, he thought, further fueling his imagination. He saw one Cheyenne who seemed to linger, slow to retreat, weaving in his saddle. Matt waved to Dow to follow and yelled, "Try to get him alive!"

Dow brought his horse to a sliding stop, spun it, and took off after the trailing Cheyenne.

The Cheyenne vanished from sight, and so did Dow, although the entire patrol was pounding hard after him.

Then there came a shot.

Soon Matt and the patrol rode up to where Jeff Dow stood over a dead Cheyenne who'd been shot in the back.

Matt looked around. The Cheyenne's Spencer lay in the dirt some twenty feet behind him.

Matt concluded that the Indian had fallen from his horse, dropped his gun, and been crawling for some kind of safety when Dow caught up with him.

It was a conclusion that the rest of the patrol could come to just as easily, and did. Private Lee spat within an inch of Dow's boot.

"Can I scalp 'im, sir?" asked Jeff Dow.

Matt barely controlled his temper. "Leave him," he snarled, "and mount up." He saw Windy Mandalian eyeing Dow and fingering his bowie knife. Matt almost gave him the go-ahead.

They rode on. But it wasn't long before they ran into gunfire.

It was the main force of Cheyenne, warned by the returning patrol and dug in to give battle. Matt and his men hit the ground but held their fire. A forward group of Cheyenne fell back to their main line.

"Can't reach them from here, sir," said Sergeant Olsen.

"I know," said Matt. "And they can't reach us. Let's use up some of their ammo. Have the men return the fire, but not too often. Let 'em know we're here. And shoot high."

"How're we gonna make contact, sir?" asked Sergeant Olsen.

"Don't know. Have to wait. If the chief's Hungry Buffalo, he's got a good head."

"They ain't where they used to be," piped up Private Lee.

"Moved out before the moon was up," said Olsen, "but Breckenridge and Chubb *had* to know it by two or three o'clock."

"To say nothing of Allison and Smaldoon," said Matt, smiling.

"Them too," said Olsen, returning the smile, "and one of them oughta be comin' up on the Cheyenne's ass pretty damn soon."

Maybe, thought Matt, but it might not matter. He'd been watching the distant Cheyenne, and had seen figures rise and distinctly wobble to other positions.

"They're near dead on their feet," said Olsen.

Chief Hungry Buffalo saw his braves getting weaker by the minute, and felt himself getting weaker as well. He didn't understand it. It seemed the Great Spirit was on the side of the Great White Father this time. It had been with the Cheyenne and Dakota at the Greasy Grass, but now the times had changed.

Hungry Buffalo realized the Americans were beyond the range of their rifles. He knew the Americans also had to be coming up on their rear. And he thought that if he waited much longer in this cursed region, this land of plague, his warriors would no longer have the strength to pull a trigger. He might have surrendered were it not for the consuming illness of his warriors, the signs of disfavor. If they were destined to die, it was best that they die fighting.

He ordered his warriors to charge the Americans.

Matt saw the Cheyenne rise and start forward, firing as they came. "Stay down and hold your fire!" Matt roared. "Don't fire until I give the word."

The Cheyenne staggered into range now, and slugs whistled overhead and dug up the soil before Matt's men. Matt and Sergeant Olsen hoped this first squad of Allison's was as disciplined as Olsen's own First Platoon.

Suddenly, Jeff Dow leaped to his feet, discharged his

Springfield and threw it aside, yanked his Scoffs out, and ran toward the advancing Cheyenne, firing as he ran.

The Cheyenne's return fire was feeble and inaccurate, and none of them managed to hit the crazed Private Dow.

Suddenly, Dow realized that not only had he shot off all his rounds, but he was out there all alone.

He had turned to return to his own line when gunfire from Matt's men suddenly joined that of the Cheyenne.

Dow spun, fell, and lay still.

The firing from Matt's men stopped.

But the Cheyenne still advanced.

Matt couldn't let the Cheyenne march right upon them, to point-blank range, and he was about to order "Fire!" when the Cheyenne came to a staggering halt. Their guns drooped or fell, and they themselves began to keel over.

"All right, men," said Matt, "let's get out there and try to take care of these bastards." He saw a figure marching slowly toward them from the Cheyenne lines. He thought he recognized Hungry Buffalo. "Windy," he said, "I think that's Hungry Buffalo. Tell him what's happened and what we're going to try to do." Windy nodded and moved forward and Matt turned to Olsen and said, "After Windy's got things straight, you get all the horses you can find and get everyone loaded up. We've got to get back to the post, fast."

It wasn't until then that he walked over and looked down at the body of Jeff Dow.

Corporal Hicks and Privates Gillies and Diamond also paused to look down at Dow's body. Weasel Gillies then looked Matt straight in the eye and said, "We were just trying to give him covering fire, sir."

Matt nodded. "Must've been a lucky Cheyenne bullet. Saves the army some re-up money."

nineteen _____

About an hour later, as Matt and his men and those Cheyenne who still had any strength were trying to load the infirm onto horse and travois, a squad from Smaldoon's platoon arrived to help.

Smaldoon had had second thoughts and, afraid the Cheyenne might have slipped by him to the west, he had led a squad off in that direction, just to make sure.

The new arrivals pitched in, and soon the entire village was being moved south.

They reached Outpost Number Nine by dusk, and the sick Cheyenne were carried into the officers' day room, where they were reunited with Crying Eagle.

The day room floor was packed solid, with barely room to move around, and overflowed into the officers' mess and the enlisted day room, but the Sanitary Corps and the post volunteers managed. And the Cheyenne were much more receptive

157

this time to the Sanitary Corps' ministrations, even to the point of receiving needles in their arms without flinching.

The only jarring note came when the Reverend McElroy decided it was a good opportunity to make a few converts.

But Captain Conway brought a stop to that. He ordered the missionaries either to simply give medical help or stay the hell away.

Amy Selby and a few others stayed to nurse, but McElroy and two of his most devout fellow workers took umbrage and left.

John Pickett had taken a break from the sick ward and returned to the Smaldoon quarters. He was getting tired, and that would not do. He couldn't afford to weaken himself all over again.

He'd been lying down for perhaps a half hour when Cassie entered. "I wondered where you'd gone to," she said.

"I'm going to get a full night's sleep," he said.

"That's a good idea, John. You need it." She came over and sat on the edge of the bed, smiling softly. "You know, people seeing you well and moving around, they may start to wonder what's going on in here."

"Let 'em. Wondering never hurt anyone."

Cassie sat quietly for a while, then reached out and took hold of his hand. "John. What *is* going on in here?"

He stared up at her.

She bent down and kissed him softly on the lips. He let it go on for a moment, then pushed her away.

"Maybe someday, Cass, maybe not. If it does happen, it'll be with you. But don't love me, Cass. I might not be around that long, I might not even be alive that long. You know my business. And I've got something to take care of before I can even think of anything else, much less..." He took a deep breath. "Fact is, it might come to a head real soon."

Cassie got up and strolled over to the window.

"Well, here comes something else. Wonder what *this* is?"

An ambulance had rolled in the gate and approached the orderly room, escorted by a squad of mounted infantry. But it was too dark outside to see anything clearly.

John Pickett peered out. "Who is it? *What* is it?"

"It's too dark....Oh, good, it's the paymaster, with the payroll. It figures he'd arrive in the middle of the night. They're always late. 'Bout drives Clay crazy."

"What's he got to spend all his money on?"

"It's the principle, John. Clay says it's the principle of the thing."

Jack Diamond rode slowly through the evening. He stopped a few times, but kept on going.

A lamp was lit in the widow's house, and she came out as he rode up. He looked down at her and she looked up at him.

"Jeff's dead," she said.

"Yes," said Diamond.

The widow remained impassive. "Perhaps you'd like some coffee?"

"Yes I would, ma'am," he replied, dismounting.

"Naomi's still at the post," she said, carrying herself stiffly back into the house. "Does she know?"

"Not from me, ma'am . . . but she probably does by now."

The widow's shoulders sagged. "I can't control her anymore."

"I know that, ma'am."

"A man would help."

"But not Dow."

She looked up quickly from pouring the coffee, then back down. "I've given Jeff a lot of thought. Was I as foolish as I think I may have been? It's beginning to seem like a nightmare."

"Not for me to say, ma'am."

"My name is Giselle . . . but not 'Zelly.'"

Diamond nodded.

"How did Jeff die . . . Jack?"

Diamond took a long time making up his mind. Finally he said, "Two other soldiers, or myself"—no sense in exposing Hicks or Gillies—"one of us shot and killed him."

The widow's breath caught, and her eyes widened.

Jack Diamond proceeded to tell her everything about the engagement that had led to Dow's death, and then he told her what the men thought of Dow, how Dow played around and talked about her, and finally he told her what Dow had tried to do to Naomi.

The widow was stunned into complete silence.

Diamond drained his coffee and walked out of the house. The widow sat as still as a rock. But then, ten minutes later, she heard the sound of hammering.

She walked outside. There was a lamp lit in the barn, where Diamond was doing some work.

"I'll leave as soon as I get this done, ma'am."

She looked at him steadily. "If you'd told me about Jeff and Naomi at the time, I would have killed him myself." She turned and walked away. But then she stopped and said over her shoulder, "I told you my name was Giselle." Then she was gone.

Diamond smiled, but decided he wouldn't hang around. She'd had enough for one day.

Back at Outpost Number Nine, Captain Conway was telling Matt Kincaid, "We'll start paying in the morning, Matt. No sense waiting until everyone's back. They're never all back here at the same time anyway."

"That's fine by me, sir. But tell me . . . do you know how long that girl's going to be in my office? She makes me kind of nervous."

"Ask Marlowe. He's the one keeping her there. With all this business, he's probably forgotten about her."

"Oh, jiminy," cried Corporal Bradshaw, "I forgot." And he jumped up and ran out of the orderly room.

He ran to the sutler's and found Fletcher there, as he'd hoped he might. He handed Fletcher a sheet of paper.

"I'm sorry, Mr. Cranmore, but with all the excitement . . . this came yesterday . . . or the day before . . . jeepers, I can't even remember. But here it is, the message you were waiting for. I hope the delay won't cause any problems."

Then Bradshaw turned and ran from the sutler's before Fletcher could raise his gaze from the message. Fletcher ran after him and shouted from the door, "Hey, soldier, when they gonna pay? There're a coupla fellas here what owe us money. We'd like to collect before we leave. This here message has got us headin' south real quick, so . . ."

"They're gonna start paying tomorrow, Mr. Cranmore. Tomorrow morning, first thing."

Fletcher stomped back into the sutler's store and drew his gang together.

"Wal," he said quietly, "thanks to that four-eyed bastard, we gotta do it here. In the mornin'. Now you two gals, you get the hell out there and find out where Aggie's gone to. I want her. We ain't gonna leave her behind to blab." He then smiled around at the rest of his gang. "This is gonna be easy still. Then . . . Oregon, here we come! 'Cept they'll be thinkin' we're headin' south! Hee-hee-hee!"

His cackle gave Pop Evans the shivers.

twenty _____

Payday. Tables had been lined up in the enlisted mess, and Captain Conway, Lieutenant Kincaid, and Sergeant Cohen were seated behind them, sorting through the paper money, checking the pay roster against the roster of those present at morning assembly.

"We're only gonna need about a third to a half of this money, Captain," said Sergeant Cohen. "Maybe we'd better leave the rest in the safe."

But Captain Conway, weary from the events of the preceding days, said complacently, "No, we'll keep it here. The rest of the men might ride in at any time."

Matt nodded his agreement. God, he was tired. He'd forgotten to ask Maggie about Pickett and Pickett's prey. And about the last thing he had on his mind just then was the mangy Fletcher bunch. As a matter of fact, a message had come in for him early that morning from Missouri authorities, containing complete descriptions of the rapacious Fletcher gang, and he'd yet to read it. It was tucked away in a pocket.

"Another fifteen minutes and we'll start," said Captain Conway.

Lieutenant Marlowe left the day room ward, where most of the Cheyenne were holding their own—it was pneumonia, as expected, that was complicating the measles for most of them—and visited Aggie in Matt's office.

She was glad to see him, and eagerly showed him where the disease had shown some response to the potassium iodide. That was good enough for him. The "great imitator" had finally been identified to his satisfaction; it matched everything he knew about syphilis.

Just then, Hattie and Billie came into Matt's office over Corporal Bradshaw's protests.

"There you are, Aggie," said Hattie. "Come on, we gotta get outa here, fast. We're all leavin'."

"Not so fast," said Marlowe. "I think you three should stay right here."

They started to protest, and he told them bluntly what they had and what they could look forward to if they left.

Hattie and Billie were horrified. Then the three girls exchanged looks. "Fletcher done it," said Hattie, her voice hard. "Him and Cullen, they was the first, those rotten bastards."

"Cullen? *Ray* Cullen?" Marlowe took a deep breath. "You'll stay then, till I get back?"

"Yes, we'll stay."

Marlowe left them and walked on down to the Smaldoon quarters. He knocked, and Cassie called out to him to come on in.

John Pickett was lying on the bed, staring thoughtfully at the ceiling. Cassie looked preoccupied. She glanced at Marlowe and said, "Oh, hello, doctor."

"What's this, a relapse?" he asked.

"No," said Pickett, sitting up. "Feeling fine."

"John thinks he'll be leaving soon," said Cassie, and Pickett compressed his lips.

"Oh?" said Marlowe, looking at Cassie and then at Pickett. "Well, I'm sorry, but if you must, you must. Which reminds me, that scrougny bunch is apparently getting ready to leave"—he saw Pickett's look sharpen—"and I think the leader's name is really Fletcher instead of Cranmore. And I also think Ray Cullen is among them." He was fascinated by the expressions Pickett was trying to keep off his face. "But there's more, and I don't know what to do. I think maybe I should try to keep

162

them here. I'm almost certain they're infected with syphilis. I've talked the women into staying. Scared them, really. I can treat them, though I don't know how much good it will do. But the men . . ."

"Don't worry about them, doc."

Such a hard voice. Marlowe didn't know what to say except, inanely, "Well, Cassie, I'll bet you wish Clay were here. They're about to start paying."

"Now?" snapped Pickett. "Right now?"

"In a few minutes."

Pickett strode to the window. He saw the Fletcher gang. Six were in the process of mounting and walking their horses to the gate, but Amos Fletcher, Ray Cullen, and a third man were walking toward the mess, leading their horses.

"Goddamn!" exploded Pickett. "All this lyin' around's made me careless." He grabbed his gunbelt and strapped the Colts around his hips. "You two know how to handle rifles?"

"Like a champ, John," said Cassie unexpectedly, and Marlowe nodded glumly; this medical mission was turning out to be a damned sight more violent then he'd anticipated. "Those single-shot rifles, though . . ." he muttered.

"Clay's got a repeater here," said Cassie.

"Where?" demanded Pickett, and Cassie showed him. He loaded it and handed it to her. "You keep it. Doc, you take mine, you'll like it." He threw it at Marlowe, who caught it, hefted it, snapped it up to sight along it, and smiled. "Now look out there," Pickett went on. "See those six by the gate? You cover them, cover my back, all right?"

"Cover your—?" began Doc Marlowe, but then broke it off as Cassie said, "Damn right. Go get 'em, John."

Captain Conway was about to tell Lance Corporal Enright, standing by the door, to let the first group in for payment when the door suddenly opened and Amos Fletcher, Ray Cullen, and the third man walked in with their guns drawn.

"Don't make a blessed move," said Fletcher. "Git over with them, Corporal."

Enright moved to flank the stunned and half-risen Conway, Kincaid, and Cohen. "Jes' settle on back down there, eeeeasy . . ." Fletcher and Cullen covered them while the third man covered the cooks and enlisted help that were staring from the kitchen.

Curses streamed through Matt's mind, and he leaned slightly forward, insanely tempted. . . .

"Don't do it, Lieutenant," advised Fletcher. "We're the

Fletcher gang and we've killed plenty already, don't mind killin' some more. Now you jes' push thet money over thisaway, Captain. *All* of it."

"You can't get away with this," said Captain Conway reasonably. "There are more than fifty soldiers out there, and this is their month's pay you're trying to steal. They'll tear you to shreds!"

"No they won't," said Fletcher, "not with you three officers as hostages."

"And how long do you think that will last?"

"Long enough. They won't chase us, knowin' your life's on the line. Now push thet money bag over here."

It was done. Fletcher leafed through the contents. "Where's the rest?" he demanded, scowling.

"That's all there is," Conway said.

Fletcher looked back at the money, then at Cullen, then at Conway. "How much is here?"

"About fifteen hundred dollars," said Sergeant Cohen, and Matt Kincaid added, "Chickenfeed."

Fletcher almost went berserk. "You're goddamn right it's chickenfeed. This is all there is? What the hell do they pay you dumbies?"

"The army's *rich*, goddammit," growled Cullen. "There's gotta be more."

"There are only a hundred men on this post, Fletcher," Captain Conway said calmly. "That's all they need to send us."

Fletcher seethed. "One hundred men," he speculated. "How much is that each man?"

"Privates only get thirteen dollars a month," Matt replied.

"Thirteen?!" Fletcher spread his lips in kind of a smile. "Then let's say this is for all the poor, dumb privates in the world. Jesus! Now, on your goddamn feet!"

They came out of the mess three abreast, with Conway, Kincaid, and Cohen being prodded along in front of Fletcher, Cullen, and the third man.

There were a number of soldiers loosely congregated outside the mess.

"Clear the hell out," shouted Fletcher, "or your captain, your first officer, and your first sergeant is gonna get their heads blown off. Now *move*."

The men, after a moment's shock, moved, and quickly, leaving John Pickett standing alone confronting them, guns still sitting on his hips.

"Who the hell are you, goddammit?!" yelled Fletcher. "Didn't you hear me? *Move!*"

Pickett didn't bat an eye.

"The name's Pickett," he answered slowly. "You're dying, Fletcher, right where you stand."

Pickett's voice had carried over the entire parade, electrifying all those who heard, except Sergeant Chubb, who was crawling along the top of the post walls, trying to get into pistol range.

Fletcher stared at Pickett. With their guns rammed into the backs of their hostages, none could get a clear shot. Why the hell didn't those bastards by the gate open fire?

The answer was that they'd seen Cassie and Marlowe lined up on them, and had enough sanity to realize that all hell would break loose if they started shooting. The only chance was for Fletcher and the other two to push their way clear with their hostages.

"You're gonna get these officers killed," said Fletcher.

"That don't mean dogshit to me," said Pickett, at the same time making eye contact with Kincaid and Conway and catching flickers of understanding. "They ain't *my* officers. The only thing that meant anything to me was my family, Fletcher. And for what you did to them, all of you are going to die." Pickett gave a barely perceptible nod.

"Yeah? An' how—" Fletcher began.

Kincaid, Conway, and Cohen flung themselves forward and down. At the same time, Pickett's red-hot hatred was bringing his guns out and up like greased lightning.

His first shot actually took the captain's hat off as it passed by to bore a hole in Amos Fletcher's gut. His second and third shots froze Cullen and the other man upright. Then he calmly pumped another slug into each of the men, finishing them.

In the meantime, Cassie and Marlowe, in front of Smaldoon's quarters, had opened up on the men by the gate. And Chubb was throwing slugs down as well.

And Matt's guns were clear before he hit the ground. He came up firing.

Most of the privates had scattered or flattened themselves with the first move, and Matt had a clear view of the six men by the gate. So did Captain Conway and Sergeant Cohen, both of whom were cursing foully.

The whole battle lasted ten seconds at the most.

Fletcher, Cullen, and the third man were dead, and the ones

by the gate were either dead or badly wounded.

There was a sudden hush as the gunsmoke rose and the dust settled.

In the silence, John Pickett strode the distance to the gate and, walking from one man to the next, shot all six men in the head. A thin, bitter smile was about his mouth.

Captain Conway was beginning to get red in the face. A fight was a fight, but he didn't care for murder, and he was damned if he'd permit—

John Pickett saw the danger signs and said, "Every one of these men is wanted, Captain, dead or alive. I wanted them dead. Besides, they're all carrying disease. The doc knows about it. They've been spreading it all over Missouri, Kansas, Illinois, and Wyoming. They're better off dead. And the women are carrying it too, so you'd do better to spend your energy checking around to see which of your men have spent any time with them."

Captain Conway glared at John Pickett, then asked, "Where's Marlowe?"

"Over here," came Marlowe's voice from across the parade.

Conway turned and strode in his direction. He was passed by Cassie, running toward Pickett.

She got to him at the same time Matt Kincaid did. Matt stood close and said, "Nice move, Pickett. Cut it close, but nice. But I don't think the captain appreciates getting all those holes in his hat."

"Captain Conway's peeved pretty good," Sergeant Cohen said, coming up behind them. "I recognize the signs. I think you'd better head out of here, Pickett."

Pickett nodded, and his whole body slowly slumped, seemed to grow weary.

His head swung slowly toward Cassie. He said dreamily, "Gotta go to St. Louis first, pick up what's left of my family, sell the farm, then . . ." He smiled at Cassie gently. "Ever seen Frisco?"

By the time Captain Conway had gotten through discussing the disease with Marlowe, Cassie and John Pickett were mounted and on their way out the gate.

Matt Kincaid walked up to Marlowe and the captain. "Pickett said goodbye, sir, and he sent you his thanks, Doc."

Captain Conway stared at Matt. "Goodbye? What the hell made him pick up and take off like that, Matt? He could have hung around for a drink, at least."

"He shot your hat off, sir."

"Oh, yes, that's right, he did . . . the bastard. . . . Well, then, if we're not going to drink, Matt, let's get back to paying the men."

Jack Diamond was seated across the kitchen table from the widow Bennett.

It was a hell of a difficult thing to work up to, but he finally got it out. "I'm afraid I've got to know when the last time was that you and Jeff Dow was . . . uh . . . was in bed together?"

The widow blew her stack. "How *dare* you!" she said, along with a lot of other unflattering things.

Finally she simmered down and ended with, "And why in the world should I tell *you*, Mr. Diamond. What business is it of yours?"

Diamond sighed. He knew it was going to be hard, probably impossible. He decided to get it out as fast and clean as he could. "I don't know if you know what syphilis is, ma'am," he said, staring down at the table, "but it's bad, real bad, a killer, and it's passed when men and women, you know, *do* things. Some girls back at the post had it. And Jeff was with them. And I been checkin', and the earliest he could've picked it up—and I understand it's near impossible *not* to catch it—would have been—" He named the date and almost the exact time.

He then stood up, and with a last look at the white, rigid face of the widow Bennett, he left.

twenty-one ━━━━━━━━━

A few weeks later the Cheyenne were well on their way to recovery. In fact, a certain number were already healthy and strong enough to travel, and were about to depart for the reservation.

Among them were Hungry Buffalo, who hadn't been as badly infected as most, and Crying Eagle, who'd been the first to receive treatment.

In a show of confidence, Easy Company's command was permitting them to return to the reservation without an escort, which Hungry Buffalo recognized as an honor.

Then, in a further show of confidence, Matt Kincaid handed both Hungry Buffalo and Crying Eagle, who was now numbered among the tribal council, each a rifle.

Hungry Buffalo received his with good grace, recognizing and appreciating the further honor.

Crying Eagle, though, noted that the rifles were the single-shot army Springfields, not nearly as good as the Spencer repeaters they'd previously wielded. The Americans were undoubtedly keeping those good rifles for themselves.

As the Cheyenne rode out, Matt Kincaid noticed the Sanitary Corps wagons being readied for travel.

"Where are *you* going?" he asked Marlowe.

"Back to the reservation," said Marlowe. "At a discreet distance, of course, so they won't think we're an escort. But they've still got to learn to use latrines."

And Marlowe and the Sanitary Corps rode out.

About an hour later, Mr. Smaldoon and the second squad from his platoon finally rode back in.

"Goddamn it, where the hell's my sister?" he shouted, emerging from his quarters. "You let that bastard run off with her?" He suddenly grinned. "Goddamn! 'Bout time."

In the meantime, Matt Kincaid was having his problems keeping Eleanora Culloch, now fully recovered, at arm's length. She seemed to think there was something special between them. And there was—namely Amy Selby, who'd let the missionaries leave without her. Amy had a new goal, a new project on which to expend her considerable energy: Matt Kincaid.

And finally, the widow Bennett showed up, with an indefinably different Naomi in tow. The meeting with Jack Diamond was difficult.

"I wanted you to know, Private Diamond—"

"Jack."

"All right . . . *Jack* . . . I wanted to thank you. I appreciate all you've done for us . . . what you . . . talked to me about, and . . . after thinking about it very carefully, I . . . well, at least I know I'm clean, if you know what—"

"I know," said Diamond quickly.

"Thank God," said Giselle Bennett, and she relaxed. "Anyway, I just came by to let you know that."

Diamond thought about it, and a rare gleam came into his eye. He smiled gently and said, "Am I to take that as an invitation to drop by sometime?"

A blush began to move up the widow's neck. Naomi giggled. The two of them began to move away.

Diamond realized he shouldn't have said anything, and began to scuff the ground in awkward embarrassment.

But the widow, after moving off a short distance, stopped, turned back to him, and said clearly, "Yes, Jack Diamond, it is."

SPECIAL PREVIEW
Here are the opening scenes
from

EASY COMPANY
IN THE BLACK HILLS

the next novel in Jove's exciting
new High Plains adventure series

EASY COMPANY

coming in August!

one _____

The rising sun spread its golden hue across the vast meadow. The lush grass sparkled with dew-slick vitality while the warmth of a new day swept a thin veil of morning fog from the upper reaches of timber flourishing along the creek. But there was no warmth in the eyes of the two warriors facing each other across the small fire that sent a frail wisp of pale smoke upward to be lost in the cloudless blue sky.

Beside the fire, a war lance had been speared into the ground; its shaft had an odd twisting curve to it that might have indicated a useless and discarded weapon. Such was not the case with this lance, however. The lance was decorated with the bright blue striping on the shaft, and twin eagle feathers were attached just behind the partially buried blade. The lance seemed to have symbolic meaning for the two warriors seated nearby in cross-legged silence, and particularly for the one on the left, whose face was marked with jagged lines of blue that crossed his forehead, ran down his high cheeks, and nearly touched at the point of his chin.

173

A feather hung limply from the rear quarter of his knotted black hair, and his muscled arms were folded across his chest, which was bare in spite of the morning chill. There was a strange handsomeness to his rugged face in spite of its stone-cold expression, and his years would have been marked near the number twenty-five.

The warrior across from him wore no warpaint, and there seemed to be a weariness about his demeanor, as though his forty years of life had taken their toll. He wore a buckskin vest and twin eagle feathers hung from his hair, but the look in his eyes was one of compassion and a plea for understanding.

Seventy-five young warriors, lean, bronzed, and sinewy, were ranged in a circle about the two, and each wore blue stripings of warpaint similar to the younger Indian's markings. They waited in silence for their two leaders to speak.

The younger man continued to stare sullenly across the fire until his hand snapped from his chest and a long finger jabbed toward the lance.

"Have you forgotten the meaning of that, Straight Shooter?" he asked without taking his eyes from the other's face.

Straight Shooter's head turned slowly toward the lance and he looked at it in momentary silence before saying. "No, Iron Crow, I have not. It is the symbol of the Crooked Lance Society, the most fierce and brave of all the Cheyenne warriors." Then his eyes drifted back to Iron Crow's face. "Have you forgotten that the Society no longer exists?"

"I have not forgotten that I am a Cheyenne warrior and that I was a member of the Society before the elders like you caused us to flee our hunting grounds and hide like squaws and little children," Iron Crow snapped, his eyes ablaze with anger. "The Society will be reborn, and we"—his arm swung in an arc to indicate the braves standing around them—"will give it meaning again. I have scars on my chest from battle and I fear no white man."

Straight Shooter smiled almost patiently. "Then you are a fool, Iron Crow. The white men are many, and more come each day. We can no longer beat them in combat."

"And what would you have us do, Straight Shooter? You were once a great warrior of the Society and a chief of the Cheyenne. What would you, in all your great wisdom, have us do while our hunting lands are stolen from us?"

"I would have us go north and join with Sitting Bull and abide by whatever decision he makes."

Iron Crow threw his hands up and a sneer curled across his lips. "Sitting Bull is a Sioux, and cannot even lead his own people, let alone Cheyenne warriors of the Crooked Lance Society! His spirit is broken and he cowers here in Canada and moans about the loss of his land and his treatment at the hands of the white people. Eventually he will become even more frightened and turn his people in to the Yellow Legs and beg for their mercy."

Straight Shooter nodded in agreement. "Perhaps, and that might be the best thing for all of us to do. The great days are gone and we cannot stay here forever. We must accept our fate and live with what we are given."

"Accchhhh!" Iron Crow snarled while spitting viciously toward Straight Shooter's moccasins. "The great days are not gone, only great warriors! Look what we did to Yellow Hair at the Greasy Grass! We defeated the finest soldier they had and destroyed his entire army. It was a great victory and one we will live again one day."

Straight Shooter shook his head. "You are wrong, Iron Crow. It was a great mistake. We took Custer by surprise and our warriors outnumbered his soldiers by four to one. What we did at the Greasy Grass will haunt us for the rest of our lives. The White Mother in England has ordered us to leave Canada, but Sitting Bull is the one the Yellow Legs want, not you and me. We are nothing to them, and once they have him and the other Sioux, we will be taken one by one until we are all dead, if we do not surrender with the great Sioux chief."

"You speak the words of a dying woman, Straight Shooter. We, the Crooked Lance Society, will return to the Paha Sapa and take what is rightfully ours. We have great medicine and the Yellow Legs will run from us in fear."

A humorous, quizzical look crossed Straight Shooter's face. "You have great medicine, Iron Crow. From where do you get such medicine?"

Iron Crow smiled in cruel triumph. "From him," he said, pointing to a man standing just behind the elder Cheyenne. "From White Claw, our medicine man. He has spoken with the gods and they have told him of our great medicine. White Claw! Tell the old woman what you have told me."

The ring of warriors moved to one side to allow passage for the medicine man, and a tall, almost emaciated Indian stepped forward. He too was in his mid-twenties, but in that lay his only similarity to the others. The right side of his face was splotched with pale, cream-colored markings, and his right eye was pinkish in color, in contrast with the deep brown of his left. His right arm was held stiffly by his side, and it too was a tapestry of white and brown that led to a hideous, grotesquely disfigured hand. The fingers of that hand were joined together and drawn in to form a permanent, curling hook that was nearly pure white. A medicine bag hung from his neck, and a long stick encased in rattlesnake skin was held in his left hand.

A singsong chant escaped White Claw's lips as he moved forward, and its sound was something like that of two coarse rocks being scraped together. His countenance and manner were trancelike as he stopped beside the fire, and his eyes were locked in the distance, as though a vision were there for only him to see.

Straight Shooter looked up at White Claw; there was no respect in his eyes. "This is your medicine man?"

"Yes he is. White Claw has great powers and he was sent by the gods to protect our people."

"I know of White Claw," Straight Shooter said, ignoring the medicine man. "He is the son of a white trapper and a Cheyenne woman. The white people would call him an albino, and they would know, as I do, that he has no powers. He is nothing more than the product of bad blood and he has been crazy since the day of his birth."

"He is not crazy, old man! He is a visionary and he has great powers with the snake stick in his hand. Show him, White Claw, and then he will know."

Slowly, as if he had heard a distant voice, White Claw turned toward the fire while the sound of his increased chanting fractured the still air. His body hunched over and his legs began to move in a shuffling dance and the feathers attached to his calves rose and fell in rhythm to the chant. As the volume of his singing increased, so did the speed of his dance, until he suddenly straightened and screamed while thrusting the stick toward the fire. The flames burst into a flash of light that lasted for several seconds before dying again, while White Claw stood frozen over them with shadows playing across his twisted face.

Straight Shooter watched in silence, obviously unimpressed, then turned again toward Iron Crow while the startled murmur of the warriors surrounding them slowly died. "May I have a look at the snake stick with which White Claw performs such magic?"

"No, you cannot." Iron Crow snapped. "No one touches the snake stick but White Claw. Silence now, old man, the great medicine man is hearing words from the gods."

Straight Shooter looked up again and listened while the medicine man threw his head back and stared up at the sky and intoned: "Maheo, the Great Spirit, we listen to you and do as you command. We will return to the land of our birth and take the Paha Sapa from the evil whites. You will protect us from Wendigo, the Great Evil One. Turtle, the great God of Life, will be with us, and Owl, the God of Death, is on our side. The white man has stolen from us and we will kill him as you have said we should. You have given us great medicine and your children will do as you command. You will guide us to victory, and the white devils will feel the wrath of Wendigo and Owl. We will have vengeance, and victory will be ours!"

And then White Claw was gone, moving through the warriors, who stood aside, watching him in awe as he walked alone across the meadow.

Iron Crow folded his arms across his chest once more and stared again at Straight Shooter. "White Claw has great medicine and we will do as the gods have told him we should do."

Straight Shooter stood and turned to face the warriors nearest him. "Now hear me!" he said in a strong voice. "White Claw is nothing more than a liar and a fake. He would lead you to your deaths against the white man to avenge his own hatred of the white father whose blood has disfigured him. White Claw is crazy, a liar and a fake, as is Iron Crow. I have come to lead you back to—"

Iron Crow's shoulder slammed into Straight Shooter's ribcage, and the older man sprawled onto the grass. Iron Crow stood over him, and his face was livid with hatred. "You have challenged my honor, Straight Shooter, and for your words you will die. You will fight me in the tradition of the Crooked Lance Society, and if you win my warriors will follow you. If you lose they will go with me to make war on the white man and reclaim our hunting ground in the Paha Sapa. Get up now, and die like a Cheyenne warrior."

Straight Shooter scrambled to his feet while Iron Crow snatched the lance from the ground and held it horizontally across his chest with his hands spaced on the shaft. The older warrior hesitated, then wiped his hands on his leggings and stepped forward to grasp the lance. He flexed his fingers on the rounded wood and stared into Iron Crow's hate-filled eyes.

"You are a coward, Iron Crow, and you are crazy. No matter what happens here, the others will know and they will follow you out of fear, not respect. If I were twenty years younger, you would be dead before you could draw your next breath."

"Those are brave words, Straight Shooter," Iron Crow said while the sneer returned to his lips again. "But you are no longer a warrior and you deserve to die."

"I am prepared for that," Straight Shooter replied, and his lips pressed tightly together while he braced his feet. "Whenever you are ready."

Their hands were locked to the shaft, and the muscles bulged in their arms with the testing strain. Then, suddenly, Iron Crow twisted the lance while kicking out with a foot to trip his opponent. Straight Shooter checked the sudden surge and stepped to one side while twisting the lance in the opposite direction. The sun was well up now, and sweat glistened on their bodies while they struggled on the matted grass for control of the weapon. They fought in silence, with only strained grunts breaking the calm, while the other braves watched from the circle surrounding the two combatants. Nearly fifteen minutes went by before youth began to take its toll on age and the lance moved more easily in response to the urgings of Iron Crow.

"You are getting weaker, old man," Iron Crow panted as he sidestepped the thrusting blow directed at his legs by Straight Shooter's instep. "Your time has come."

Straight Shooter did not reply, but he could feel the strength draining from his arms, and the sweat on his palms was making it increasingly difficult to control the violent twisting of the lance. Another ten minutes passed and Iron Crow was beginning to tire as well; the determination on his face had replaced taunting words. He was surprised by the strength of the old warrior, who was fighting now on nothing more than courage and pride. A plan was slowly forming in Iron Crow's mind, and even though he knew it was a violation of the unwritten rules of the Crooked Lance Society, he also knew he could not afford to lose a test of strength to the old warrior.

In one sudden motion he jerked the lance toward his chest, drawing Straight Shooter inward. Then, dropping to his back on the grass, he curled his legs up and caught his opponent in the stomach with his feet. He pressed upward and back, and

Straight Shooter catapaulted over his head to land sprawled upon his back.

Iron Crow leaped to his feet and whirled just as Straight Shooter scrambled to one knee. He swung the heel of the lance to crack the weapon sharply across the other man's jaw. Stunned, Straight Shooter flipped onto his back and Iron Crow closed in with sweat streaming off his face and streaking the blue paint that dripped onto his chest. His chest rose and fell in gasping heaves, and he stared down at the man lying at his feet while raising the lance to strike a killing blow.

Straight Shooter's eyes cleared and he looked upward with no indication of fear as he drew in tortured breaths.

"Do you . . . wish to . . . beg for your . . . life . . . old man?" Iron Crow gasped.

"Never. You . . . are not only a liar and crazy . . . you are also a coward. You don't deserve to . . . be called a . . ."

The lance blade flashed in the sunlight an instant before slamming through Straight Shooter's throat and sticking into the ground behind his head. The old warrior opened his mouth to speak, but his jaw hung down and his eyes slowly closed.

Iron Crow turned away to rest his hands on his knees and gulp in several breaths. When his strength returned, he pulled the lance from Straight Shooter's neck and brandished the blood-red weapon high above his head as he turned to face the warriors, who watched him silently and with a hint of disgust.

"We will kill the whites and take the Paha Sapa!" he screamed. "We will kill them with no mercy, as Straight Shooter was killed! Any warrior who wishes to challenge my leadership, step forward now!"

His cold, taunting eyes searched out the faces of each man before him until they all slowly shook their heads and turned away. Iron Crow smiled in triumph. "That is good. Get to your ponies now! We go south to take what is ours!"

As Iron Crow walked toward his mount, a man, heretofore unheard from, lowered the brass object he had been polishing in his hand and stepped toward the warrior. "Nice work, Iron Crow," he said. He was a man of stocky build, medium height, and wearing fringed buckskin trousers tucked inside his boots. A tattered blue army coat covered the woolen undershirt across his chest. A Schofield Smith & Wesson hung from his hip, and the black belt and holster around his narrow waist matched the color of his skin. There was a pleasant, unperturbed look on his ebony face while he placed the brass object comfortably beneath his left arm before adjusting the broad-brimmed hat to a more comfortable position over his kinky hair.

"I won, that's all that matters, Black Devil," Iron Crow returned. "Are you sure you know how to use that thing?" he asked, nodding toward the man's left arm.

Willy Harper smiled at the Indian's reference to his adopted name. Having served his time with the Union Army during the Civil War, he had seen his share of battle and rather liked being called Black Devil.

"I do," he replied in response to the Indian's question. "If I didn't, I wouldn't be here."

Iron Crow studied him more closely. "We are depending a lot on you and what you say you can do for us. You and your Yellow Leg sergeant friend. Are you sure his information is correct?"

"You mean about the new outpost being built near Eagle's Nest Pass?"

"Yes, that is what I mean. Is it?"

"Absolutely. It's being manned by a greenhorn cavalry outfit that hasn't ever looked down the workin' end of a barrel. If just plain scared ain't enough, we'll have them so confused that they'll cut and run, and you and your braves will have no trouble pullin' off another Little Big Horn. And as far as the outpost itself goes, it'll burn like a tipi in a pitch fire. The folks that built it didn't know a hell of a lot about what they were doin'. The ones that are garrisoned there know even less."

Iron Crow cocked his head and a curious look came into his eyes. "Why do you want to become involved in this?"

"You know the reason. Me and Sarge already made a deal with you on that."

"The gold?"

"The gold."

"I don't know why the yellow metal is so valuable to your kind, but we do have an agreement. But what I want to know is, why do you wish to make war against your own kind?"

Harper grinned, and white teeth flashed in his black face, which was partially covered by a scruffy beard. "Them ain't my kind. I'd wager I got more reason to hate the white man than you do, but you could never understand my reason why. Let's just say I got tired of pickin' cotton, bein' called a nigger, and takin' orders from white folks. The only thing they respect if you're a black man is money, and when this deal is through I'll have plenty of that."

"Money? What good is money? The hunting land of your father is the only important thing."

Now the grin widened. "My father ain't never had no land. And the only thing he ever hunted was possum. There ain't many of them 'round here. Now, what say we cut a fat hog in the ass and head south?"

A puzzled look filled Iron Crow's eyes in response to Harper's last statement, and he watched the black man for several seconds before shrugging and swinging onto his pony's back.

Harper was still smiling while his foot found the stirrup to his McClellan saddle. A Spencer repeater hung from the spider attached to the right front swell of the saddle, and a shiny saber was attached to the left. As Iron Crow urged his horse to the front of the mounted warriors, Harper took up the rear and softly blew an old Southern ballad on the gleaming brass bugle in his hand.

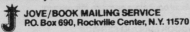